Murder At Taurus

A Lunar Enforcement

Mystery

by

Paula F. Winskye

Liam,
Merry Christmas
2021
Paula

This book is a work of fiction. All the characters, situations, & events in this novel are products of the author's imagination. Any resemblance to persons, living or dead, is purely coincidental.

Cover photo: Public domain by Apollo 8 astronauts.

Chapter 1

Jared Pearce gazed through the skylight of his apartment at one of the few things he loved about his job. Earth floating in a sea of black. He never tired of the view.

Seated on the bed, he slipped on his weighted boots, then strapped on a thick belt containing his weapons and handcuffs before adding a heavy vest identifying him as a Lunar Enforcement Officer. Chief, to be exact. He completed his outfit with weighted gauntlets.

On Earth, the gear would add one hundred and fifty pounds to his two hundred pound, six-foot-four frame. Here on the moon it brought him to a whopping seventy pounds. Still, it meant less time in the gym with resistance weights in the never-ending battle to maintain muscle tone and bone mass.

He slid open the door and smiled at the reason he had lived on the moon for the past three years. His wife Dr. Karen Mason-Pearce, in her blue Sequent Mining jumpsuit. Neither fat nor dainty, Karen described herself as "big-boned." He thought she was just as beautiful as the day she first tackled him on a high school football field.

The Lunar Governing Board had lauded his qualifications for the job of Lunar Enforcement Chief: twenty years as a Naval

Criminal Investigation Service special agent—six as agent afloat on an aircraft carrier. There were similarities to the five lunar settlements.

But Sequent Mining really wanted Karen and her PhD in Geology. So they convinced the other three corporations and NASA to hire him for the newly-formed Law Enforcement Division.

Jared supervised a force of twenty officers spread among four bases. NASA had private security, though he coordinated with them, visiting Armstrong base once a month.

He kissed Karen, who handed him his "Sippy Cup" of coffee. Spills were a real problem in low gravity.

"Thanks. So today's the big moon walk."

Karen beamed. "I don't know how much walking I'll do. It's just so much easier to inspect the crushing operation from a rover."

"Don't give me that. All you science geeks will get down and hop around the surface like a bunch of little kids."

"I still can't understand why you don't enjoy that."

"Because I have to wear a space suit. It's bulky and clumsy." He flashed a crooked smile. "And if my nose itches, I can't reach it. I'll be happy when they develop a rover that lets you travel from one base to another without a space suit."

"I suppose if I had to do it every other week, like you do, the novelty would wear off. You just hated it right from the start." She wrapped her arms around his neck. "Have I told you lately how much I appreciate this sacrifice you made for me?"

He encircled her waist and shrugged. "I'm getting paid an obscene amount for the easiest law enforcement job *ever.* But, remember, ten years. No more."

Karen brushed the gray-streaked brown hair off his forehead. "I may be ready to go home before then. Especially if we start having grand babies. So what are your plans today?"

"Walk my beat. Have lunch with Halolani and Marek. Speak to the eighth grade class about law enforcement careers."

"Busy day."

"The dangerous job of a LEO."

She rolled her eyes and gave him a quick kiss. "I'd better get moving." She grabbed the rolling case containing her space suit and touched the panel beside the front portal. It slid open, admitting her to the bright hallway.

Jared ate breakfast, refilled his coffee cup, then left the apartment. The glass-enclosed walkway separated residences and businesses from the dome's interior containing the base farm.

He knew it was not really glass, but some polymer that could withstand meteor impacts. He used the nearest portal to enter the farm, his favorite spot. A rooster's crow made him smile.

"Bonjour, mon ami," a man called from near the chicken coop.

"Morning, Henri."

Henri Le Claire, the farm manager, opened the coop door and the birds flew out. Not in the awkward way chickens flew on earth. Jared had to dodge two. Some landed in the fruit trees and others made it all the way across the hundred meter enclosure.

The first fowl had come to the moon a decade ago as eggs. Because of their short generation span, they had evolved, growing longer, more usable tails and becoming better fliers than their earthbound cousins.

Jared walked a path between rows of carrots and beets to join Henri. "What's new?"

"I am arranging a trip to Taurus next week."

"You just *have* to see the goats."

"I am delivering corn stalks. They are slow to compost and the kids could use the roughage. Tani Dai has requested corn stalks from all settlements. Once milk production starts, they will share cheese with all."

"There probably won't be enough to buy it in the store."

"Sadly, no." Henri shook his head, causing a strand of black hair to fall into his eyes. He brushed it aside. "I am afraid we will need to make a reservation at *Earth View* if we want fresh cheese."

"I can't wait. Are you feeling okay? You look tired."

"I *have* been tired lately." Henri laughed. "I think I am letting excitement over this trip keep me awake."

"You can sleep during the rover ride. I'd better make my rounds." Jared left the farm through another portal.

Rover buses ran daily between the four commercial bases. In addition to Sequent's titanium mine on the northwest shore of the Sea of Tranquility, Tani Dai collected Helium 3 in the Taurus Littrow Valley, Aqua Luna mined ice at the North Pole, and Lunar Adventures brought wealthy tourists to the Apennine Mountains.

For the average Earthling—short of winning a trip—the best way to get to the moon was to be very good at your job. A sign welcomed new employees at their temporary quarters. "Only the Best Work Here." Many fulfilled their one-year contract, making about four times what they would for the same job on earth plus free room and board, then returned to the big blue marble.

Jared greeted the employees at the barber/beauty shop, processing center—lunar speak for butcher shop—and the bank. No one needed money here. Any purchases were made with a retinal scanner. The bankers helped residents with loans and investments on Earth.

He left his pod, home to couples with no children eighth grade or younger, and used the above ground walkway to the central dome. All the bases, except NASA's, were set up like a five spoke wheel, with the rim invisible from the air. It consisted of underground tunnels connecting one pod to the next.

Jared preferred the natural light of the spokes. He picked and ate a handful of grape tomatoes from the planter running along one side of the walkway.

Vegetables grown in the walkways were free to any resident who cared to gather them. Some people preferred to buy their produce from the store. Others ate all their meals at the cafeteria. He had never gone home empty-handed when he set out to pick vegetables.

A portal opened to the central dome and the smell of perspiration wafted in the air. Behind the bleachers of a regulation-size soccer field about fifty people worked out on resistance weights, stationary bicycles, and other equipment with adjustable tension. The place was busy day and night.

He chuckled. The terms were relative. Lunar day and night lasted about two weeks each. The moon operated on a 24-hour Earth day based on Greenwich Mean Time, the universal time code. He crossed the artificial turf of the field—water was used to produce food—and entered another spoke. Peas grew in the planter along this walkway.

It took him to the temporary housing pod. New employees sometimes lived here while they waited for an apartment to open up. And workers installing equipment stayed here. Slightly more humid than the other pods, different plants grew in the central dome, including citrus trees. This was also home to the cafeteria, general store and a climbing wall.

He used the tunnel to move on to the singles pod with a bar, dance club, and racquetball courts. Its central dome held a pond. Gentle waves lapped at the beach on one side. Nut trees and personal gardens for those who preferred growing their own food filled the rest of the open space.

Lunar Enforcement, Tranquility Precinct, received most of its calls to this location. *Hormones and alcohol, a volatile combination.* No one was ever arrested more than twice. A second arrest resulted in mandatory banishment from the moon and its high-salary jobs. He could count on one hand the people he had been forced to remove. The citizens were very well-behaved.

Jared headed down another spoke, picking and eating several green beans. He cut through the central dome again, entering a spoke lined with cucumber plants. Digital posters on the opposite wall informed him that Tranquility's soccer teams would play the North Pole Polar Bears this Saturday.

Everyone who was not working attended the school's soccer matches. Music concerts, speech contests, and spelling bees attracted the same crowds. What else was there to do?

Jared entered the "families with children/school/infirmary" pod.

"Hey, Chief." Halolani Makai waved. Her dark skin and black hair attested to her Hawaiian ancestry. She attracted attention, even wearing the weighted vest.

"Good morning. Where's Marek?"

"I think he's dealing with some low-grav sickness. Open places really seem to bother him, so I told him to patrol the tunnels and walkways."

Jared sipped his coffee. "I hope it doesn't take him long to adjust."

"It's been two weeks. I was over it by then."

"It took me a couple months."

She laughed. "Yeah, but you're old."

"Keep it up, Sergeant, and I'll bust you down to officer." He smiled. All of his officers kidded him about his age, though his fiftieth birthday was still a few months off. "Let's go educate some kids."

Chapter 2

The school and playground occupied the center of this pod. Like most other things on this base, the ten classrooms were arranged in a circle, with the middle occupied by the kitchen, lunch room, and common area.

Jared knocked on his friend Gordon Sheldon's classroom door. The native of Australia taught sixth, seventh, and eighth grade social studies, health, and physical education. He also coached the fifth/sixth and seventh/eighth soccer teams.

For the next half-hour Jared and Halolani spoke about their diverse law enforcement experience, then answered questions from the ten eighth-graders. He had done this many times, both on the moon and when his own children were in school.

All lunar students were polite and respectful. Parents were responsible for the behavior of themselves *and* their children. An unruly child could get parents banished too, though it had never happened.

Jared and Halolani left the room to the sound of applause. He let his breath out. "Let's see how Marek's doing." He touched the communication device hooked over his ear. "Enforcement Two-One, this is Enforcement One. Report."

Within seconds. "Enforcement two-one. In the tunnel between the farm and corporate."

"Meet you at corporate."

"Copy that."

Jared passed through another sliding door and descended a ramp into the tunnel decorated with students' artwork. They emerged at the Sequent Mining reception desk.

This pod had a different arrangement. The two tunnels and walkway from the hub all opened into the lobby. He looked around for Marek without success.

They exchanged pleasantries with the receptionist before Jared's newest officer entered, pale and unsteady.

"Marek, it will get better."

"That's what people keep telling me," the compact officer said with just a hint of an eastern European accent.

"Have you had a chance to see the view from here?"

"No." Marek looked like he might throw up.

"Corporate is one of the few places with a clear view of the surface. This way."

Jared and Halolani took the hallway around the offices with Marek trailing.

Beyond the glass, the Sea of Tranquility spread out before them. The crushing plant lay to their right. They could see the lunar equivalent of an "off-road" truck hauling a load of iron ore to the growing mountain. After separating it from the titanium ore and oxygen, they could only pile it, waiting for the day when it would be economically feasible to export to earth.

Several rovers zipped around. Jared guessed that Karen occupied one of them.

He turned his attention to Marek, with his back against the inside wall, and offered an understanding smile. "My first two months, I was on the verge of a panic attack most of the time."

Marek's eyes widened. "You know?"

"You're not sick. You're scared to death."

Halolani looked from one to the other. "You're kidding."

"No." Jared shook his head. "I only came because Karen wanted to. I figured after all the years of following me around, sometimes to places where they didn't need a geologist, I owed it to her. I *did not* trust this glass. No matter how indestructible they claimed it was."

"Yes." Marek nodded vigorously. "The only place I feel safe is the tunnels. And our apartment."

"It *is* safe. In twelve years there's never been a breach."

"I know. It doesn't help. We came here to get out of debt faster. Anna is doing fine. I just can't shake my fear. Suggestions?"

"You don't have to do this alone. Tell Anna what's going on. I didn't talk to anyone, including Karen. She was having so much fun I didn't want to ruin it for her. I had to figure this out myself. Two things. Work out. It will keep you busy and give you less time to think."

"And?"

"Sex."

Halolani rolled her eyes. "*Men.*"

Marek grinned. "Really?"

Jared nodded. "Lots and lots of sex. Trust me."

Marek chuckled, more relaxed already. "Thank you, Chief."

"Don't mention it. Now, let's get some lunch."

***

After lunch, Jared left Halolani and Marek on patrol while he climbed the steps to his office on the second floor of the corporate pod. It actually had a better view than the ground floor, but the tiny space could handle only two people.

"Hello, Rita."

A computer screen image appeared on the wall and a female voice spoke. "Good afternoon, Chief." Everyone personalized their computers. He had chosen a female voice and given her the name.

"Are there any meetings on my agenda?"

"Tomorrow at 1000 Zulu you have a video conference with the General Manager of Lunar Adventures concerning a new exhibit at the museum."

The hub of the L.A. base contained the Lunar Exploration Museum, which could be accessed from either side without mingling of humans or the air they breathed.

"What exhibit?"

"A Soviet-era Luna probe."

"Is all the paperwork in order?"

"Paperwork? You *are* a relic, Chief. All documentation is in order."

Jared had also programmed Rita to joke with him. "That meeting shouldn't take too long. Bring up the new personnel files."

The screen filled with a Lunar Adventures passenger manifest. All of the newcomers would be in isolation for two days. They had already passed through a twelve-day quarantine on Earth, followed by the half-day space flight.

Lunar Adventures transported personnel and tourists in different shuttles. Tourists never came in direct contact with lunar personnel, other than some of the L.A. employees.

Rita recited the manifest details. "Fifteen full-time and five temporary personnel arrived by shuttle this morning and are currently in quarantine. The temporary workers are bound for NASA's Armstrong base. One full-time worker will be stationed at Tranquility base, seven at Taurus, three at North Pole, and four will remain at Apennine."

"That's a big group for Tani Dai. Are they expanding?"

"Tani Dai Corporation plans to increase their personnel at the Taurus-Littrow Valley base by five percent before the end of their fiscal year, bringing the population to seven hundred, fifty-five."

"They may catch up to us before long."

"At the current rate of expansion, the Taurus-Littrow base will reach the current population of the Tranquility base one year and four months after the end of Tani Dai's fiscal year."

"Thanks, Rita. Let's see the personnel file of the new Sequent employee."

Marguerite Boyle's picture and personnel file appeared on the wall. In her fifties, Boyle hailed from Maine. She would be working in Sequent Mining's shipping department, coordinating the export of titanium to Earth.

"Rita, set up a lunch meeting with her after she's been here about a week."

"Yes, Chief."

"This is the first time in months that I've only had one newcomer to meet. Since that's all I have, I guess I can get to know the other new arrivals better. Let's see the rest of them."

Reviewing the files filled up the remainder of his afternoon. "That will be all for now, Rita."

He grabbed a woven basket from a cabinet and left the office. Even though he could have reached his apartment through one tunnel, he used the spokes, picking cucumbers, tomatoes, and green beans. He took those home, retrieved a grocery bag and used the nearest tunnel to reach the store.

It resembled stores on Earth. All the day-to-day essentials could be found here. Shelf-stable food came in vacuum-sealed packets rather than cans or bottles. He could purchase lunar-grown fish, poultry, eggs, and produce. Other meats came frozen from Earth. Jared purchased chicken breasts, fresh bread from the bakery, and lettuce.

The young cashier smiled as she began ringing up his purchase. "You must be cooking tonight, Chief."

"Doreen, sometimes you just want to stay home."

"I hear you."

Jared paid with the retinal scan and jogged back to his apartment. He secured his Taser and Immobilizer in the bedside stand, an old law enforcement habit. The front door would only admit their housekeeper at her scheduled time, him, or Karen. No one else could enter without being invited or two keys and an override from environmental control.

"Hola, Carmen. ¿Hay algún mensaje?"

The household computer responded, not in his earpiece, but from above. "Hola, Chief. Tienes tres mensaje. La primera es de Kyle."

Their younger son's voice came. "Hi, Mom and Dad. We got eight inches of snow last night, so this weekend I'm going home with Tom and we're hitting the slopes. Love you both. Oh, I aced the chemistry exam."

"El segundo es de Joel," Carmen said.

Their older son spoke in an excited tone. "Hi, Mom and Dad. I love you and I'll be seeing you soon. I was selected for the Air Force Lunar flight next month. I'm the only applicant who's been there, so thanks for that. We're hoping to break the speed record by a few minutes and we'll practice landing and docking at all the bases, staying overnight at each one. My CO is making arrangements for each of us to speak to the school kids. That will be a new experience. You'll know more when I do."

Jared grinned. A visit from one of their kids was worth celebrating.

Carmen spoke again. "El último mensaje si de Kayla."

Their daughter sounded tired. "Hi, Mom and Dad. Just called to say I love you. I'm between meetings. Gotta go."

"Thanks, Carmen. Save the messages, but rearrange them. Put Joel's last."

"Oh, we are speaking English now?" Carmen still had a Spanish accent.

"I have to think too hard to speak Spanish. But you can play Spanish guitar music. The soothing kind."

Jared put together his salad, slid open the refrigerator door, and switched it out for the chicken.

"Carmen, grilled chicken breasts."

The cooking surface began to glow. He dropped the chicken on the surface, then sanitized his hands before seasoning the meat. He placed the green beans in a clear container, spritzed them with water, and covered the dish before setting it beside the chicken.

"Steamed beans."

He used a tongs to turn the chicken, then brushed the vegetable trimmings into an opening at the back of the counter. When he closed the cover, a soft whirring sound told him that the compost had been vacuumed away to collection bins.

"Dr. Mason-Pearce is just leaving the corporate pod," Carmen said.

"Thanks, Carmen." He removed wineglasses from the cupboard and squeezed red wine from a pouch before walking to the door.

Karen smiled when she saw him. "Wine. What's the occasion?"

Jared handed her a glass and kissed her as the portal closed. "Listen to the messages." He returned to his preparations while she did. When Joel's voice came, he turned to watch her.

First, Karen grinned. Then, she giggled. Then, she set her glass aside and leaped into the air, nearly hitting her head in the low gravity. Jared caught her when she landed and they shared a long kiss.

"Oh, Jared. He said it was a long shot to be selected for that flight."

"Joel has never believed in counting chickens before they hatched. Yes, there were a lot of qualified candidates, but none with lunar experience. I always thought there was a good chance. And this time when he visits, we won't have to talk to him through glass. He'll have gone through quarantine. Dinner's ready." He kissed her again. "If I had listened to the messages before I shopped, we could have gone out to celebrate."

"That's okay. I like it when you cook."

Chapter 3

The next morning, Jared decided to get a later start. "Carmen, play the local news."

He sat at the table with his breakfast and the television screen appeared on a convenient wall.

The female anchor smiled. "Good morning, Lunarians and visitors. I'm Regina Gonzales. It's Tuesday. Today's weather is sunny with a temperature of 120 degrees Celsius. Don't go outside without your spacesuit." She grinned. It was her daily joke. "Sunset will be in about eleven Earth days.

"In breaking news, next month the International Air Force will attempt to set a new speed record for a moon flight. A crew of eight will leave Earth orbit en route to Armstrong base, and will spend twenty-four hours at each settlement before the return trip. Some familiar names are among the crew members.

"Mission navigator will be Lieutenant Wanda Kim, daughter of Drs. Sara and Shin Kim of North Pole. And Lieutenant Joel Pearce, son of Dr. Karen Mason-Pearce and Chief Jared Pearce of Tranquility will be the flight engineer.

"I'll have reaction from those parents later this week."

Jared sighed. *Another interview.*

"Welcome to those new Lunarians still in quarantine. With your arrival, the population has surpassed thirty-five hundred for the first time.

"You've told us that you wanted more, and here it is. New video of the baby goats at Taurus."

Jared had to admit that he enjoyed watching the kids make spectacular leaps.

The anchor's face appeared again. "Here's the Lunar Network programming for today. Up next. 'Exercise to maintain bone density and muscle mass,' followed by 'Lunar Gardening,' then 'Taurus Children's Concert,' and the replay of Saturday's soccer matches between the Apennine Mountaineers and the Taurus Bulls.

"And don't forget, this Saturday you can watch a live broadcast of the North Pole Polar Bears and the Tranquility Sharks matches."

"News off."

The screen disappeared and Jared finished dressing for work. He stopped to visit with Henri at the farm again. "So, when's the big day."

"Monday."

"You'd better get some rest before then. You look tired." Jared headed for the central dome. "Good morning, Rita. Where's Lars?"

Her voice came in his ear. "Good morning, Chief. Captain Larson is leaving the cafeteria en route to the hub."

"Thank you." He entered the dome seconds before his senior officer, as blond and fair-skinned as one would expect of a Norwegian. They had arrived on the same flight three years earlier. "Morning, Lars."

"God dag, Jared."

"Anything I need to know about?"

"All is quiet."

"Wait till Friday night."

"Perhaps I will need my bullwhip." Lars patted the handle of his Immobilizer.

The weapon had earned the bullwhip moniker because it required the same skill to operate. A cord shot out, encircling the troublemaker, resulting in a roughly five-minute paralysis. Larger miscreants could start to move in as little as two, so an officer needed to apply handcuffs quickly.

The latest in non-lethal force because it could knock down even those immune to Tasers, it had a loyal following on Earth. On the moon, where traditional firearms were out of the question, Jared had ordered them for all his officers.

"Walk with me." Jared took the spoke to corporate. "Don't count on it. Everyone has seen the videos. They respect these things."

"Ah, well. I can always wish. How is the new fellow doing?"

"Scared to death. I gave him some advice on how to deal with it. Did you see the news this morning?"

"Yes. Congratulations. You both must be so excited."

"It's pretty stellar. We had decided that if any of the kids wanted to visit again, they'd have to pay their own way. Joel gets a free trip. And not only that, we don't have to talk to him through glass. Want to meet for lunch?"

"Do you mind if Lena joins us?"

"Not at all. I'll see if Karen's free. I don't think the girls have had a chance to visit in awhile."

***

Jared and Karen had the weekend off. They watched the soccer games from the packed bleachers, dined at *Earth View* Saturday night, attended church services by video Sunday morning, and spent the afternoon rock climbing.

Monday morning, they returned to their routines.

Jared again started his day with a visit to his friend. "So today's the big day."

Henri smiled. "I delivered the corn stalks and my suit to the rover bay. As soon as my assistants arrive, I will be on my way. Hiro told me yesterday that the kids have begun leaping from the top of Mount Fuji."

Jared smiled. The Japanese corporation had built their central dome over a eight meter high rock and given it an appropriate name. "They're adapting well."

"Indeed. The experiment seems to have worked. Within a few months they should be having kids of their own. We are far from self-sustaining, but every victory brings us a step closer."

"Probably won't happen in our lifetimes. When will you be back?"

"Tomorrow afternoon."

"I'll miss you tomorrow morning. Have fun."

Chapter 4

On Tuesday, Jared patrolled with Marek. His new officer had a little more color in his cheeks.

"Is it helping?"

Marek flashed a crooked smile. "Some. After I talked to Anna, she was happy to help. I've slept without medication the past two nights. And if I spend enough time on the weights, I'm so tired it's hard to feel anxious. But I'm exhausted."

"Once you're comfortable, you won't have to work out so much. My other piece of advice ..." He chuckled. "You won't need that as much either. Your choice."

"We'll see how soon she gets tired of me."

Rita's voice came in Jared's ear. "Call from Lieutenant Carter at Taurus."

"Go ahead, Lonnie."

"Chief, I'm afraid I have an unattended death here."

Jared halted. In the twelve years since lunar settlement, there had been five accidental deaths witnessed by multiple employees. Only two unattended deaths. You had to be in excellent physical shape with no pre-existing conditions to work here. Lunarians *did not* drop dead.

"Who is it?" Jared had reviewed personnel files and met every resident.

"I'm afraid it's a friend of yours. Henri Le Claire."

Jared leaned against the nearest wall. "Henri. I just saw him yesterday."

"I'm sorry, Chief. I've secured the scene and Doc Yamato is on her way to examine him now. What do you want me to do?"

Jared took a deep breath to give himself time to think. *You can do this. Just follow protocol.* "I'll arrange for a shuttle. I can be there in a couple hours. Have Doc take samples, but keep everyone else out of there. We'll transport Henri back here for autopsy."

"I'll take care of it."

"Rita, end call. Call Dr. Klein. Urgent."

The request yielded fast results. "Klein here. What's happening, Chief?"

"I have an unattended death at Taurus. You'll get the body later today for autopsy."

"That doesn't happen very often. I'll be ready."

"Doc, it's Henri."

"No-o." Dismay filled his voice. "He just had his physical last month. He passed with flying colors."

"I know."

"I'll review his file. Don't worry. I can handle this. When you have a more definite time, I'll free up the scanner."

"Thanks, Doc. Rita, end call. Call transportation services. Urgent."

Again, the connection came fast. "Good morning, Chief. What do you need?"

"I have an unattended death at Taurus. I need to get there in a hurry."

"I'll page the shuttle crew. Estimated time to departure, thirty-five minutes. Bring your suit to the shuttle bay."

"I'll be there. Rita, end call." Jared stood staring at nothing for a moment.

"Can I do anything, Chief?" Marek asked.

Jared focused on him, noticing that all traces of fear had vanished. He nodded. "Rita, Officer Dorshak will come for the forensics kit. Give it to him."

"Yes, Chief."

"Okay, Marek, meet me at the shuttle bay."

"Copy that. I didn't know you could get a shuttle on demand."

"I can. And only a handful of others have the authority. But shuttles are expensive to operate. I've only done it twice before. I'm going home to get my suit. Rita, call Karen."

***

Jared stowed all of his uniform accessories in a travel bag so he could fit into the shuttle seat. Ground crew members locked his space suit case in the rear of the vehicle.

Once the second officer sealed the hatch, the ground crew left the air lock and it retracted from the shuttle. The two-man crew completed their pre-flight check and fired up the engines. Retro-rockets lifted the craft from the surface and away from the settlement at a slow, steady pace.

When the captain pushed a lever the main engines drove Jared back into his seat. Though not as fast as the plasma-powered inter-planetary vehicles, the shuttles cut travel time from hours to minutes.

In an instant they left the Sea of Tranquility behind, flying over the Sea of Serenity. After all of his rover trips, he knew the landscape as well as anyone.

He identified the snake-like Dorsa Smirnov off to his right. Moments later, the Apennine Mountains rose from the surface, with the Lunar Adventures settlement on the slope of a wide valley.

His mind wandered to Henri. *What happened? Henri has been here more than ten years. He founded the farm. Does something go wrong with your body after you've been here too long?* Jared shook his head. *Doc said everything checked out a month ago. We have to figure this out. Not just for Henri, for all of us.*

"Chief," the captain said. "We're approaching Taurus."

"Thanks."

The shuttle slowed and began its descent. It touched down with a slight bump and the station airlock extended.

The captain unbuckled his harness and stood to face Jared. "Chief, what are our orders?"

"Wait here. Later today, I'll need you to fly the body back to Tranquility for autopsy, accompanied by one of my officers."

"You're staying here?"

"Until I complete my investigation. I don't know how long that will take, but I'll get another shuttle from here."

When the second officer opened the hatch, Jared grabbed his gear and bounded through the airlock. Lonnie, as tall as Jared, but slender, met him inside.

"Report." Jared handed him the forensics kit, then dropped his bag on a bench and began replacing all of his weighted accessories.

"Amaya has the scene secure. Doc Yamato is analyzing the samples she collected. She saw no signs of trauma, like if Henri fell."

"How do you fall hard enough to kill yourself on the moon?"

"I thought of that."

"Who found him?"

"I did. Hiro Tanaka was supposed to have breakfast with him before Henri left on the rover. When he didn't show, Hiro went to Henri's quarters. When he got no response, he requested a locate. Tracking showed Henri in his quarters. I got called for a welfare check. I got there about the same time as the woman from Environmental Control and we used our keys to open the door."

"Lead the way. What did you see?"

Lonnie strode along the hallway and down the ramp leading to a tunnel. "He was sitting in the lounge chair. It looked like he just fell asleep and didn't wake up. No sign of a struggle or distress."

"Did you touch anything?"

"I checked his carotid for a pulse. Other than that, I followed protocol. No matter how remote the possibility, we treat it like a crime scene. I reminded Doc of that when she arrived. I had to turn my back when she took her samples, but I assume she followed protocol too."

Jared nodded. He also got a little squeamish when medical personnel extracted vitreous humor. "Did Doc Yamato get the data from Henri's health monitor?"

"Yes. Henri stopped breathing at 2324 Zulu. His heart stopped a couple minutes later."

They climbed a ramp and doors opened into the temporary housing pod.

"Was Henri with Hiro last night?"

"Hiro and his family, until about 2130. Then Henri said he was tired and would see him in the morning."

In the corridor ahead, Jared saw officer Amaya Ito, just five feet tall, guarding the door.

She turned toward them. "Morning, Chief. Sorry about your friend."

"Thanks, Amaya." He tossed his bag against the base of the wall. "Have Environmental Control get me a room. Both of you, wait here."

He took a deep breath and used the retinal scanner. Once Lunar Enforcement took control, any officer could gain access to a room.

Henri reclined in the lounge chair of the studio apartment just as Lonnie had described. He had changed from his day clothes and poured a glass of wine. Knowing Henri's habits, Jared estimated that he had consumed about half.

"Computer T-34, list viewing history beginning at 2130 yesterday. Authorization LE One."

"Yes, Chief." A female voice responded. "At 2145, occupant requested Earth News, southern France edition. At 2215, occupant requested chamber music. At 2300, with no further requests, I shut down the player."

"Did anyone else enter the room since Henri Le Claire checked in?"

"Yesterday, at 1715, Hiro and Ichiro Tanaka entered. At 0820 today, Lunar Enforcement Officer Lonnie Carter entered. At —"

"That's enough. Any unusual fluctuations in the habitat's environment since the occupant checked in?"

"Upon his arrival at 1620, the occupant requested that the temperature be raised two degrees. At 1645, he requested that the temperature in the turbo shower be lowered five degrees."

Jared's brow furrowed. Henri liked his showers scalding. If he had been interviewing a human, he would have questioned the response. But the computers never misspoke.

"Thank you, Computer." He pulled on gloves. "Rita, call Lonnie."

"Calling Lieutenant Carter."

"You ready for me, Chief?"

"Bring in the forensics kit. Have Amaya come in, too."

Lonnie entered and placed the kit on a table. Jared opened it. He handed Amaya the finger print scanner. "The housekeepers wear gloves. If they did a good job, the only prints in here should be from after Henri's arrival. But start with Henri's possessions so I can bag them."

"Hai, Chief." Amaya began running the scanner's beam over every surface.

"Lonnie, collect the wine and any other consumables. I'll check the trash." He grabbed a bag from the kit. "Computer T-34, save the compost bin from this room for analysis."

"Yes, Chief. The bin currently has compost from nine rooms. Diverting additional compost."

"Return the trash."

"Please, place bag over opening."

Jared found the hatch under the kitchenette counter and held the evidence bag over it. "Ready."

Air pushed the bag open before minimal items blew in. Henri had spent little time in the room.

"Return complete."

Jared sealed the bag and examined the contents. Two wine pouches. *Henri always has a glass after a trip and before bedtime.* A sushi package from the Taurus store. *He always has fresh sushi when he comes here.* And a medication packet. Jared used a magnifier to look for writing. He found none. *What were you taking, Henri?*

He placed the bag beside the kit and turned to Henri's travel bag. In addition to the expected items, he found two unopened medication packets, also unmarked. He collected them.

"Lonnie, get the compost. There shouldn't be much from nine guest rooms."

Jared gathered Henri's possessions, separating the items Henri had unpacked from those still in the travel bag. Then, he unfolded a body bag.

When Lonnie returned, all three enclosed Henri in the bag. Jared pushed a button and the bottom of the bag stiffened to make it easier to carry.

"Do either of you want to volunteer to take the body back to Tranquility? You'll probably have to stay overnight."

"I contacted the rest of the team," Lonnie said. "Takeo offered to go. He's ready."

"Call him."

Chapter 5

Jared struggled with his next move. Should he keep working the scene or escort his friend's body to the shuttle. In the end, he chose the latter.

When Takeo arrived at Henri's room, Jared gave him evidence bags containing anything Henri had consumed, including the unopened medication. "Give this to Doc Klein. I'll take a shuttle from here tomorrow and you can ride home with them."

"No rover. My kind of trip."

"And you get to see your girlfriend."

Takeo dropped his eyes, smiling. "You know about that?"

"It's a small town. I know everything. Lonnie, finish up here, then take the rest of the evidence to the lab. I'll be back as soon as the shuttle lifts off."

When he returned from the shuttle bay, Lonnie and Amaya waited outside Henri's room.

Lonnie reported. "We found Henri's prints, along with Hiro's and his son's. And an unidentified thumb print."

Jared just stared for a moment. "That can't happen."

"That's what we thought. But Rita confirmed that it's not in the system."

"Where did you find it?"

"On Henri's shaving kit."

"Henri hasn't been off-world since November. A print left there three months ago would be smudged by now." He chewed his lower lip. "Except that he put the shaving kit away when he got back and didn't take it out till yesterday. Have Rita check all the Earth databases."

"She's already working on it."

"Good. Let's secure the scene." He opened the door. "Computer T-34, admit no one without verification from two Lunar Enforcement officers."

"Room secured."

"Lonnie, you're with me. I want to talk to Hiro. Amaya, resume your other duties."

"Hiro told me we could find him at the hub," Lonnie said.

Jared knew the way. He took the nearest spoke to the hub of the Taurus settlement. Like Tranquility, food grew in planters along the walkway, in this case pod peas.

When the doors slid open, he heard a goat, though he could not see Mt. Fuji through the forest of bamboo.

They followed a winding path and the bamboo gave way to cherry trees. He saw rock just before they cleared the trees and reached a pond. The goats, almost full-grown, scrambled across the sides of Mt. Fuji in a game of tag.

Jared surveyed the landscape around the pond—more rock than plants—but manicured. He saw Hiro on a bench near a shrine. They crossed a bridge and reached him via another winding path. Jared waited a moment, hoping Hiro would notice him.

"Hiro."

The fortyish man turned. "Jared." He rose and bowed, then took Jared's hand in both of his. "I have been waiting for you. I will miss him so much."

Jared swallowed hard. "That makes two of us. You've known him a lot longer than I have."

"Eight years. He was my mentor for lunar farming. We video-conferenced every day. Do you know what happened?"

"Not yet. I need to ask you some questions."

"Please, have a seat. Or we can go someplace more comfortable. I came here because this was Henri's favorite place."

"This is fine." Jared selected another stone bench. "Rita, record. Hiro, you were Henri's best friend. Are you aware of any medication he was taking?"

"Medication? Other than the occasional patch for a headache or sore muscles?"

"Yes."

"He never told me about anything. Are you sure?"

"We found one open packet and two others. They weren't marked."

Hiro rubbed his chin. "Do you think he was keeping a condition from us? Something that would have kept him earthbound?"

"What do you think?"

"The moon—his farm—was his life." He nodded. "This was his home. It would have broken Henri's heart to stay down there, looking up. You know that most years he only used a week of his vacation there?"

"Yes. He spent a week here and a few days at each of the other bases. Always learning."

"If his condition killed him, he died as he wished. I cannot be saddened by that."

"We'll have to wait and see. Take me through yesterday."

"He called me a little after 1600 to say that he had arrived. I told him I would come get him at 1715. Ichiro accompanied me. We visited for a few moments in Henri's quarters, then came here. We discussed agriculture and watched the goats for some time. At 1830, we returned to our apartment, where Hoshi had prepared dinner. Afterward, all five of us played mahjong. Henri seemed tired. He excused himself at about 2130 and said that he would see me this morning."

"No one else became sick?"

"No. The children are in school. They do not know about Henri. This will be difficult. They have never lost someone close to them."

Jared nodded. "I'll need a list of everything Henri ate and all of Hoshi's ingredients."

"Of course. I doubt there was anything she had not served him many times. He had his favorites."

"Henri loved food. Did he talk to anyone else while you were with him?"

"He greeted many people. There were many others at Mt. Fuji and three stopped to visit with him. Claude de Gaulle, Toshiro Fudo, and John Simmons."

"How did he know them?"

"Toshiro, you may remember, is one of my farm workers. Claude comes from the same region of France as Henri. They often reminisced when Henri was here. John took several of Henri's lunar gardening classes. He never missed the chance to ask questions."

"Did Henri ever tell you anything in confidence? Something that I wouldn't know."

Hiro looked away. His eyes grew misty. "Ah-h ..."

"You can't harm him now, Hiro. He was my friend too. If it had nothing to do with his death, it goes no farther."

Hiro glanced at Lonnie.

Jared turned to his officer. "Give us some space, Lonnie. Rita, stop recording."

After Lonnie retreated a suitable distance, Hiro sighed. "Henri married young."

"I knew that. He said it didn't work out."

"In truth, he abandoned his wife and daughter. Later, he made financial restitution, but the child never forgave him. He never forgave himself."

Jared nodded. "Now I understand. He always looked a little sad when he told people to treasure their children."

"Yes. I am also certain that he never told you this. In his youth, before he even married, he was involved in a radical group."

Jared caught his breath. "That would have disqualified him from this job. If I had known, I would have had to report it."

"We spoke of that. He knew that you would not let the knowledge affect your friendship. However, as a man of honor, you would have also done your duty. You should check Henri's will. If he had any other secrets, they may be revealed there."

"I'll do that. Anything else?"

"The other secrets he shared with me, he also shared with you. He considered you a close friend, Jared."

"Yeah." He gazed at the goats, coming down to the pond to drink. "He knew a farm boy when he saw one." He stood. "I may need to speak to the rest of your family. But I'll contact you before I do."

"Of course." Hiro stood and bowed. "How long will you be here?"

"I don't know. At least overnight." Jared found Lonnie again. "I'm going to my quarters to watch Henri's will."

"Anything I need to know, Chief?"

"Like most of us, Henri did some stupid things in his youth. Why don't you go grab some lunch."

"Want me to bring you something?"

Jared walked in silence for a moment. "Talk about a tough question. I'm not really hungry, but I suppose I should eat. Chicken and vegetable stir fry."

"Chopsticks?"

"Yeah."

They parted ways and Rita guided Jared to his quarters. He entered a studio apartment identical to the one Henri had occupied.

"Computer T-26, hot tea."

"More input required."

"The local favorite." He found a cup and placed it under the beverage dispenser, then took the tea to a lounge chair but remained standing. "Rita, play the last will and testament of Henri Le Claire."

"Multiple files found. File names: Will, Rachelle Le Claire, Hiro Tanaka, Jared Pearce."

Jared sank into the chair. "Play the file with my name."

Henri's image appeared on the wall. "Jared, my friend. How do I begin? Thank you for being a dear friend. You are a man of honor and integrity. And, for that reason, I found it necessary to lie to you. I am truly sorry. I reveal all now.

"In my late teens I became involved in the *Cause Vertueuse.* Blame youthful rebellion or a charismatic leader, it matters not. I left home, met my future wife, and—though I never committed atrocities—I turned a blind eye to them. Until I became a father. I tried to convince Michelle to leave. She refused.

"You see, my father-in-law was the charismatic leader. Michelle told me that she would not stop me, but if I left, it would be without her and Rachelle. I hung on for another month. Then, I could take no more. I started a new, peaceful life.

"Ten years later, when the governments of the world said 'Enough' and cracked down on all the extremist groups, Michelle and her parents were killed. Rachelle and the other children were made wards of the state. If I had come forward to claim her, my involvement would have come to light and ruined my future. And, coward that I was, I chose to remain silent. A year later, she was adopted by Michelle's aunt and uncle. I offered them financial support, which they accepted. But Rachelle never forgave me. She has had a good life nonetheless.

"Now you know. More than once, I wanted to confess to close friends. I resisted, because the truth could block so many opportunities. I had long dreamed of living on the moon. I studied all agricultural subjects which could make me useful there. When they began building the first settlement, I applied, and was hired. My dream came true.

"And I loved it more than I ever imagined. So a confession was out of the question. I could not give it up. Since you are seeing this, I have passed. I hope that it happened on my precious moon. Thank you, and good bye, my friend."

Jared wiped his eyes and just stared at Henri's image until the room's computer startled him.

"Officer Carter requests admission."

"Rita, close file. Computer, open door."

Lonnie entered, handed Jared the food container, and pulled out a chair by the room's small table. "Did you learn anything?"

"More details about what Hiro told me in private."

"You still don't want to share it with me?"

"It's need to know. If it becomes important to the investigation, I'll tell you. Let's listen to his will. Rita, play the Henri Le Claire file labeled 'Will.'"

Again, Henri's image appeared on the wall. "Bon jour. I am Henri Jean Charles Le Claire and this is my last will and testament. I leave my mother's jewelry, my wedding ring, and all of the money in my various accounts to my daughter, Rachelle Le Claire. I leave my collection of agriculture and gardening texts and files, along with my personal gardening tools, to my good friend, Hiro Tanaka. And, I leave my Napoleonic Era French Army sword to my good friend, Jared Pearce, who I also name executor of my will. All my other possessions he may donate to charity, or distribute as he wishes. This concludes my last will and testament. Thank you."

Jared stared for a moment. "Rita, close file."

"Did you know?" Lonnie asked.

"That I was executor. I had forgotten. He said that he had updated his will about a year ago and named me. He also told me about the sword because I had admired it."

"I didn't know he had a daughter."

"Neither did I. Hiro told me. She and Henri were estranged."

"Are you going to eat?"

"I suppose I should." Jared used the chopsticks, speaking between bites. "When I finish, we'll see if the lab has learned anything from the evidence."

Chapter 6

Jared could have video-conferenced with Dr. Yamato and the lab technicians, but he needed the walk. In the Taurus habitat, the infirmary and lab shared the same pod as the gym and soccer field.

The lab portal opened when they approached. Lunar Enforcement officers had access to restricted areas in all the settlements.

A receptionist looked up from her desk. "Good day, Chief, Lonnie. Is this in regard to the evidence from this morning?"

Jared just nodded.

"I will contact Dr. Yamato." After speaking to the doctor for a moment, the receptionist stood. "This way."

They followed her into a hallway to the first door on their right. Dr. Yamato rose from her desk, the top of her head barely reaching Jared's shoulder.

"Gentlemen, please have a seat." She waited for the door to close behind the receptionist. "The blood and vitreous humor samples yielded some unexpected results. Mr. Le Claire's blood contained therapeutic levels of the drug Rutac HCL. It is an anti-seizure medication. There is no mention in Mr. Le Claire's medical records about a seizure disorder. If he had such a disorder, he should have been earthbound."

Jared nodded. "And I'm guessing that's why there's nothing in his medical records. The moon was Henri's life. He must have found a doctor on Earth to prescribe the medication, off-the-record."

"Unwise. However, I do not believe that a seizure killed him. Rutac is very effective at the levels I found. Mr. Le Claire seems to have died of oxygen deprivation. Blood oxygen levels were too low to sustain life."

"He suffocated?" Jared scowled. "How?"

Dr. Yamato held up her hands, palms up. "Perhaps the autopsy can determine that. Did anyone hear him complain of drowsiness?"

"Yes. Hiro said that he looked tired, then excused himself for that reason. And I noticed a couple times during the past week that he looked tired."

"I believe that was due to slowly dropping oxygen levels."

"If he hadn't been alone, could he have been saved?"

"That depends on the cause. I have never heard of these symptoms except in an enclosed space, when the subject slowly used up the available oxygen. Carbon dioxide poisoning, as it were. Again, the autopsy may reveal more."

"You said you found something in the vitreous humor."

"An unknown substance. Of course, there is no such thing. That does not change the fact that it is not in the database. The lab is conducting a chemical analysis as we speak. Once we have its makeup, we should be able to determine the symptoms it would produce."

"Contact me as soon as you have that information."

"Of course."

"Anything useful from the other evidence?"

"No anomalies attracted our attention. However, we are not forensic scientists. I will send you our findings. Samaru, send the evidence file from today's Lunar Enforcement case to Chief Pearce."

"Hai," the computer replied.

Dr. Yamato formed her fingers into a peak. "Do you want us to release the evidence to you or hold it?"

"Hold it for now." Jared stood. "I'll take it when I go back to Tranquility. Thanks, Doc. We'll let you get back to your work."

***

Jared assigned Lonnie to arrange interviews with the other three people Henri had conversed with. He returned to his quarters to listen to the rest of Henri's will.

"Rita, play Henri Le Claire file named Rachelle Le Claire."

Henri's image again appeared on the wall but Jared immediately noticed the time stamp. This had been recorded in December, not a year ago like the others.

"Rachelle, my precious Rachelle. The days I spent with you last month were the best I have had since I left those many years ago. Thank you for forgiving me. Thank you for introducing me to my grandson. I have treasured our daily talks.

"Since you are viewing this, I have passed. I hope we enjoyed many years together."

"Rita, pause file." Jared took a deep breath, then wiped his eyes. "Henri, that's why you were so happy when you came back from vacation. I'm sorry you didn't have more time with her. Rita, resume."

"I have few possessions, my dear, however there have been few expenses these past ten years. I have acquired a tidy sum. I already created a trust fund for Jacques. The rest, I leave to you. You are also the beneficiary of my life insurance policy. I leave you my wedding ring and my mother's jewelry. She wanted you to have it one day.

"Rachelle, know that you have brought me so much joy. I love you. Till we meet again."

"Rita, close file. Where will I find Rachelle Le Claire?"

"On Earth. Nice, France."

Since Nice was near Greenwich, Great Britain, the longitude on which Zulu time was based, Jared knew that he would not be calling her in the middle of the night.

"What's her schedule?"

"Today is a holiday in France. Her office is closed."

"Try to contact her at home."

The connection to Earth always took a minute. Jared moved to a chair at the table, in front of the room's camera. Rachelle Le Claire appeared on a screen below it. A man moved into view, standing behind her.

"Bonjour, Chief Pearce. You are my father's friend, no? Is something wrong?"

"Yes, ma'am. I'm his friend. And, I'm very sorry, but there *is* something wrong. I'm afraid that your father passed away in his sleep last night."

"No." She reached up. Her husband took her hand and kissed the top of her head. "How? I thought one had to be in perfect health to live there."

"We're still investigating. And you're right. There are rigorous health requirements. When I know the cause, I'll tell you. I'll need to ask you some questions, but not now. May I call you tomorrow?"

"Yes. Of course. I will take the day off work. You may call me here."

"Thank you. If you have any questions about your father, I'll try to answer them when we talk again."

Jared watched the file Henri had left for Hiro, then stood and stretched.

The room computer spoke. "Officer Carter requests admission."

"Let him in."

Lonnie stood in the doorway. "Claude de Gaulle has to go to work in an hour. He asked if we could interview him now."

"Lead the way. What about the others?"

"We can talk to Toshiro Fudo afterward. By then, John Simmons's shift should be over."

"After we finish the interviews, I need to contact Henri's brother."

"Ever met him?"

"Once. Henri got him one of those VIP tours a year ago."

"Really? I thought the tourists in isolation suits were all company or government big wigs."

"Most are. But, if you're willing to pay, you can actually show someone where you work."

"I'll pass. It was expensive enough bringing my folks to the hotel and visiting them through the glass."

"That's what we did with the kids. Though we got a rover and took them out sightseeing."

They found de Gaulle pacing in the lobby of Tani Dai headquarters. When he saw them, he gestured to seats away from the reception desk.

"Gentlemen, I am not sure how I can help you. I only visited with Henri for a moment yesterday."

"We won't keep you long," Jared said. "Did you know Henri before you came here?"

"I knew of him. When I was hired, I researched what other Frenchmen I might encounter. As you know, we are a small minority. Henri and I had little in common. I am IT and he was a *farmer*. But he loved good wine and good food, so we had that to talk about."

"My father is a farmer." He glared at the man long enough to make him squirm. "Did you notice anything different about Henri yesterday?"

"He did not seem to have his usual energy. Other than that, nothing."

"What did you talk about?"

"Wine and food. He tried to interest me in those dreadful goats, but I have no love for animals. I excused myself."

"Thank you. That's all I needed." de Gaulle bounded from his seat and strode away. "Jerk."

Lonnie nodded. "I've never liked him. The kind of guy who gives Frenchmen a bad reputation. Nice comeback. Toshiro is at the farm."

"Good. I need the smell of a barnyard."

"I'm spending my next vacation on a ranch. I miss horses."

"Me too. We live on a hobby farm back home."

"Who takes care of it while you're here?"

"Karen's niece lives in the guest cottage. She was working as a horse trainer at a big boarding stable but really wanted to start her own business."

"Win. Win. I gave up my apartment, so I spend my vacation traveling or mooching off relatives."

Jared smiled.

They passed through the sliding doors into the domed farm. Fruit and nut trees lined the elevated pathway. Ducks swam in the flooded rice paddies on either side. The fields occupied half the farm space, making this the most humid pod on the moon. At the end of the walkway, chickens scratched between rows of vegetables.

They found Toshiro shelling soybeans. He bowed. "Greetings and condolences, Chief. How may I help you?"

"Thanks, Toshiro. Tell me what you and Henri talked about yesterday."

"He inquired about my family as he always did. We discussed the expected soybean yields. However, the main topic of conversation was the goats."

"Did you notice anything different about him?"

Toshiro considered the question for a moment. "He *did* seem tired. I only stayed briefly. He was here to visit Tanaka-san, I did not want to monopolize their time."

"Thanks for yours." Jared exchanged bows with him and nodded for Lonnie to lead the way.

Before they reached the farm doors, Rita's voice came in his ear. "Incoming call from Dr. Yamato."

"Go ahead, Doc."

"We have the chemical makeup of the unknown substance. Analysis indicates that it would prevent oxygen absorption. Even if medical personnel had been present to administer O-2, Mr. Le Claire's body could not have used it. I have forwarded my findings to Dr. Klein."

"Is it a poison?"

"Considering that it is not a naturally occurring substance and it is lethal, it *could be* classified as a poison. The authorities on Earth should be notified as soon as we know more."

"I'll take care of it. Thanks, Doc. Rita, end call. Check with the database on Earth. See if there are any unexplained deaths with symptoms matching our case."

"Yes, Chief."

Jared passed the information on to Lonnie, then walked in silence for a moment. "Why would anyone poison Henri?"

Lonnie did not answer immediately. "It couldn't be because of anything he did here. Everyone liked Henri. His past mistakes may become pertinent to the case."

"I know. I'll think about it overnight. If I decide to share it with you, I'll expect you to keep it to yourself."

"You know you can trust me, Chief."

"Absolutely."

***

After they interviewed Simmons, Jared and Lonnie headed for the Lunar Enforcement office. On the way, Rita reported her findings.

"In Cannes, France, a man died of similar symptoms despite being treated at a medical facility where oxygen was administered."

"Was the compound present?"

"It was not detected. It is the only similar death which was placed in the unexplained database. I am checking the worldwide death notices for oxygen deprivation cases attributed to closed spaces."

"Thanks, Rita. You're a good detective."

"Thank you, Chief. Also, the unknown print found on Henri Le Claire's shaving kit belongs to Celeste Dion, a teenaged girl living in a small village in France. Her parents own a bed-and-breakfast where she works as a housekeeper. He stayed there."

"Why did it take so long to find?"

"The village maintains its own fingerprint database. It is difficult to access. Incoming call from Dr. Klein."

"Go ahead, Doc."

"I've completed the scans. Henri died of oxygen deprivation due to his body's inability to absorb it. The lab has also detected the same compound Dr. Yamato identified in Henri's body in both of the wine pouches. They are currently analyzing the stomach contents."

"In your professional opinion, was Henri murdered?"

Silence, then a heavy sigh. "As hard as it is to imagine, yes."

"I'll have Lars collect the rest of the wine from Henri's apartment so the lab can test it."

"The wine he consumed last night wouldn't be from his private stock."

"Yes, it would. I gave him a hard time about how fussy he was. He wouldn't buy wine on the moon, except what he could get at the fine dining restaurants. He imported his favorites from France and would have packed some when he came to Taurus."

"So our murderer may be on Earth."

"That's a very strong possibility."

"Good. I feel better not wondering which of the people I know murdered my friend."

"It's too early in the investigation to eliminate anyone as a suspect. I'll probably be back there tomorrow. Let me know if you have any results before then."

When they reached the office, Jared passed all this information on to Lonnie. Rita reported again, this time her voice coming over the speakers in the room. "I found two deaths in France and another in Switzerland attributed to suffocation, possibly due to a tightly-sealed room."

"What were the ages and nationalities of the victims?"

"Fifty-one, fifty-eight, and sixty. All were French."

"Run deep background checks on all three and the previous victim you discovered. Lock the office door."

Lonnie raised his eyebrows, then took a seat at one of two facing desks. "I'm all ears."

Jared settled into the other chair. "I don't need to sleep on it. You need to know this. I've kept it to myself because it has nothing to do with the Henri we knew. When he was young and impressionable, he joined the *Cause Vertueuse.*"

Lonnie whistled. "I learned about them during my law enforcement history class. They were a nasty bunch. I don't remember what the name means though."

"Virtuous cause. Pretty sickening when you consider how many people they killed." He shook his head. "In the part of Henri's will addressed to me, he talked about the charismatic leader and falling in love with his daughter."

"That will make a man do really stupid things."

"Henri married her and they had a daughter. When his conscience would no longer allow him to stay, he could not convince his wife to come with him. He had to leave them both."

Lonnie nodded at length. "People talk about making sacrifices for what's right. Henri really knew what that meant. You think he saw something the last time he was on Earth? Maybe someone from *Cause Vertueuse* in a position they should have been disqualified from?"

"Maybe." Jared drummed his fingers on the desk. "But why would they use a slow-acting poison? I told Henri a week ago that he looked tired. If he saw someone in November, why give him months to report it?"

"Good question. We really need your experience now. You've probably investigated more murders than the rest of us combined."

Jared threw up his hands. "I didn't think my department would need that kind of experience."

"Don't beat yourself up, Chief. One detective per settlement has been more than enough. I didn't mean to sound clueless. You and me and Lars can handle this."

"You're right. I'll bring Lars up to speed when I get back to Tranquility. You both closed your share of tough cases. That's why I hired you."

Lonnie grinned. "It wasn't my sparkling personality?"

"That might have helped a little. Let's just say I didn't hire anyone who rubbed me the wrong way."

Chapter 7

The next morning Jared interviewed Hiro's family members before the kids left for school. He scheduled a shuttle for after lunchtime, then went to the office with Lonnie to review what Rita had found overnight.

"Rita, report on the background checks of the four victims."

"Jean Dubois is the only victim with an old criminal record. He had two arrests as a juvenile and one as a young adult. Of more significance, he and the other three victims seem to have vanished during the greater part of the 2040s, resurfacing in 2049."

Jared met Lonnie's gaze. "Right after the crackdown on extremists."

"Someone is eliminating former *Cause Vertueuse* members?"

"Taking no chances that one of them will name names. Rita, call Interpol Captain Julian in Paris."

"Yes, Chief."

Jared explained to Lonnie while he waited for the call to go through. "I talk to Captain Julian when Interpol does background checks on my non-American officers. She's the only person with any rank that I know there."

"You must have worked with some in your NCIS days."

"A handful. None long enough to develop friendships."

Rita interrupted. "Your call is ready."

Jared faced the camera and a very rugged woman with what could almost be described as a crewcut appeared on the wall. "Good morning, Captain."

"Bon jour, Chief. You have another new officer candidate?"

"No. Something far more important. And confidential."

Julian nodded. "Computer, lock room. We are secure, Chief."

"I need Interpol to reopen three unexplained death cases in France and one in Switzerland. I believe all four victims may have been members of the *Cause Vertueuse.*"

Julian leaned forward, forearms on her desk. "I am intrigued. But how did this come to your attention?"

"We lost a man here. Because of the health requirements, unattended deaths are rare. We insist on an explanation. He died of oxygen deprivation. Our lab found a chemical in his system which can interfere with the body's ability to absorb oxygen. In his will, he admitted that he had joined the *Cause Vertueuse* in his youth, leaving about ten years before the crackdown."

"We have always known that some extremists escaped the crackdown. On occasion through the years, I hear of one who has been exposed. Those responsible for heinous crimes are dealt with. The others are simply barred from sensitive occupations."

"They can't work here."

"Yet one did. Send me the four names."

"Rita, send the file."

Julian turned away from the camera as she studied the information. She pursed her lips and faced him again. "We are already investigating the Dubois case. We were not aware of the *Cause Vertueuse* connection."

"Rita, send the lab analysis. Inspector, our doctors believe that the unknown chemical compound is the cause of death. Have your lab look for it."

"Unknown compound? Someone has created a new poison?" She studied her computer screen again.

"It looks like it. Something that can pass itself off as natural causes. The victim was a friend of mine. The only symptom anyone noticed was that he seemed tired."

"For how long?"

"I commented on it a week ago."

"I will need his name as well."

Jared sighed. "I know. I'll ask for discretion. He left the *Cause Vertueuse* because his conscience told him to."

"He was not one who simply escaped the crackdown. I understand."

"Rita, send the file on Henri's murder. Captain, his daughter lives in Nice. I've already told her of his death. But I will be talking to her again shortly. Do you want me to tell her that he was murdered?"

Julian leaned back. "He was your friend. Do you have a relationship with the woman?"

"I didn't know she existed until yesterday. He kept more than one secret."

"Does she know of his past?"

"Oh, yes. She was one of the crackdown orphans."

"Sacre bleu!" She sat up straighter again. "Does she know you as her father's friend?"

"Yes. He spoke of me."

"Then, tell her. Tell her of the possible connection to *Cause Vertueuse*. How old was she at the time of the crackdown?"

"At least ten. Maybe even eleven or twelve."

"If someone is killing former members, she could also be in danger. Tell her that I will be contacting her personally about security. However, I want you to conduct all interviews. She knows that you care about her father. She is more likely to reveal all to you."

"Okay."

"I wish you were here. An in-person interview would be better. You know, if you ever decide to come back to Earth, you have a job here."

Jared smiled. "That would be a long commute from my ranch in New Mexico."

"We have offices in New York. That would be a shorter commute."

"A little." Jared chuckled. "But thanks for the job offer. I'll let you know what I find out."

"And I will keep you informed of developments in these cases." Her brow furrowed. "If these are victims of the same poison, the killer might have gone undetected for years if he had not struck there."

"Maybe he didn't know about the strict health requirements."

"True. If one has no desire to work on the moon, one would not research that information. I will contact you as soon as I know more."

"Thanks, Captain."

"Au revoir."

"Rita, end call." He turned to Lonnie. "Input?"

"Had you considered that Henri's daughter may be in danger?"

"The thought crossed my mind. At the time of the crackdown, she was old enough to know people. It depends on how much her mother and grandfather sheltered her from what they did. Does the murderer see her as a threat? We don't know."

"You're sure that's what's going on? A former member is eliminating anyone who could reveal that."

"You have another theory?"

"Just playing devil's advocate. The government is eliminating former members?"

Jared shook his head. "People have had enough of extremists. Governments don't need to kill them in secret. Public trial and punishment are popular."

"Okay. How about someone who lost something to the *Cause Vertueuse* and thinks they should all die?"

Jared raised his eyebrows. "Now, that's a valid theory. Yeah. If that's the case, Rachelle shouldn't be in danger. And that would also explain why the killer chose a slow-acting poison. Thanks for playing devil's advocate."

***

Rachelle Le Claire's puffy eyes marred her otherwise beautiful face. "Bon jour, Chief. Is it morning there?"

"Yes, ma'am. We operate on Greenwich Mean Time. Do you have any questions about your father?"

"Since our reunion, Papa and I talked almost every day. He often mentioned you. He preferred rural people. He said that you came to the farm almost every morning."

"Yes, ma'am. It starts my day off right."

"You are the first person I have spoken to who knew him. What was your impression of him?"

"He was kind and gentle. He loved animals and was loyal to his friends. For most of his life, he dreamed of coming to the moon. When people started planning settlements, he studied everything he could to get a job here. He was very proud to be the first farmer on the moon. And he is considered the foremost authority on lunar agriculture. People will be taking his classes for years."

She smiled and wiped tears away. "When I started searching for him, I discovered his on-line classes and took them. He was so zealous about his work, and wanted his students to feel the same. Getting to know him that way allowed me to let go of my anger. Do you know how he died?"

"Yes, ma'am."

In the pause that followed, she shook her head. "Please, call me Rachelle."

"Okay. I'm afraid there's no easy way to say this. Your father was poisoned."

She gasped and placed both hands over her mouth. "Why?"

"We're not sure yet. But there may be a connection to four suspicious deaths on Earth."

"What did they have in common with Papa?"

"They may have all been members of the *Cause Vertueuse.*"

She stiffened and her tone became formal. "He told you of that?"

"In his will."

"He did not trust you with that information while he was alive?"

"He trusted me to do my duty. He knew that if he told me, I would be obligated to report it."

"You could not keep a secret for a friend?"

"Not a secret like that. Henri respected me for it. So he left me a file in his will because he didn't want me to hear it from someone else."

Her shoulders dropped and she nodded. "He had the utmost respect for you. Integrity, he said. You think he was killed because he was once a CV member. But he left long before the massacre."

"I know. I believe the other four men were members right up to the end. They seem to have vanished during most of the forties, reappearing in 2049."

"Through my job, I understand the tracking system." Rachelle sighed. "Not even monks disappear completely for ten years. Hermits, yes. But the likelihood is far greater that they were members of a fringe group with false identities. They were all French?"

"Yes. Though one was living in Switzerland at the time of his death."

"Then your theory that they were CV members is valid."

"Did you know many CV members?"

She looked away from the camera for almost a minute. "Most of us lived on a farm, what was once called a commune. So I saw many members. I was a child. Grand-père and Maman never discussed politics around me. But the leadership often dined with us. I think they were all killed in the massacre."

"Have you seen any members since?"

"Yes. In most cases, on the news when they were caught."

"But not always."

"There are two who were discovered and only guilty of being CV members. I have sought them out so they know that not everyone hates them."

"Any others?"

"I will *not* betray former CV members. They have paid enough."

"They may be in danger. *You* may be in danger."

She stared at him. "You think this is some kind of vendetta?"

"We have two theories, both valid. Someone hates the CV so much that they want all former members dead. In that case, you *might not* be in danger. The other is that a former CV member would lose everything if another member reported him to authorities. If you knew him, he could see you as a threat."

"I know the CV did bad things." Rachelle sighed. "I know Maman and Grand-père did bad things. I am aware of two other former CV members. I will not tell you their names. Neither of them are in sensitive jobs and they are leading peaceful lives. They would have no reason to kill anyone."

"Okay." Jared chewed his lip. "Did your father see either of them when he was there?"

She hesitated. "Yes. One."

"I won't press you on this, but I want you to think about it. Someone, probably on Earth, laced your father's wine with poison. It may have been a former CV member. While he was with you, did he recognize anyone else?"

She took her time. "I am not aware of anyone. But he only spent a week with us. He had to visit his brother before he returned to quarantine."

"I'll talk to his brother also. Do you have any other questions?"

"So many. However, I want you to catch Papa's killer. Perhaps, after that, we can sit down and talk of Papa."

"I'd like that. Thanks for your time. Rita, end call." He stiffened. "Rita, call Lars. Put it on speaker."

Jared noticed Lonnie's quizzical expression.

Lars's voice filled the room. "Ya, Chief."

"Send out a bulletin to everyone. Anyone who drank a glass of wine from Henri's private stock after his trip to Earth in November should report to their clinic."

"He shared his wine?"

"Rarely. But he offered me a glass more than once."

Lonnie's eyes widened. "You didn't drink it?"

"No. I told him good wine was wasted on me. I could just contact Henri's close friends, but I don't want to take any chances."

Lars spoke again. "Do you want the bulletin for Tranquility or lunar-wide?"

"The whole rock. Henri toured the other settlements after his last trip to Earth, visiting the other farmers. He could have shared."

"Lunar news will get the bulletin. Regina has never had a story this big."

"I'll have to deal with that. Put it out. I'll give Doc Klein a heads up. He can contact the other medical teams. Have you checked with Henri's computer for any unauthorized entry into his apartment?"

"Ya. As expected, nothing. I am also watching footage of his housekeeper while she cleans. I've gone back six weeks and so far she does her job, then leaves."

"Thanks, Lars. I'll see you this afternoon. Rita, end call."

Jared stood, then after a moment returned to his chair.

"What's on your mind, Chief?"

"I wanted to pace but there's no room. And before I go walk the halls, I need to talk to Henri's brother."

"Want me to do anything?"

"Check with Hiro personally. See if Henri gave him any wine."

"I'm on it." Lonnie bounded from his chair and out the door.

"Rita, call Hubert Le Claire." He faced the camera until Henri's older brother appeared.

"Chief, have you any news?"

"I'm afraid so. Henri's death was a homicide."

Hubert gaped. "I have never heard of a murder there."

"It's our first. Henri's wine was laced with a slow-acting poison. I need to ask if you drank any when he visited."

"I drink wine from *bottles.* He has no choice but to use those pouches, but they are inferior. He drank bottled wine when he was in France."

"So he told me. That's good. I don't want any more deaths. I have some tough questions for you."

"Proceed."

"Did you know that Henri was a member of *Cause Vertueuse?*"

"Yes. I also knew that he made a great sacrifice rather than remain with them. Thank God. Or he would have died with the rest."

"While he was visiting you, did he recognize anyone?"

"Family. Childhood friends. As you would expect."

"No one who surprised you?"

"No. You think he was poisoned here?"

"The wine is packaged there. To insure authenticity, vintners seal the cases. Retail stores here open the cases and sell by the pouch. But Henri broke the seals on his cases. Someone would have had to enter his apartment to poison him here. We've checked into that. No one entered his apartment who didn't belong there."

"Of course. His computer would have informed him of an intruder."

"How many other people know that Henri was a CV member?"

"Few. My parents were so ashamed, they told no one. Rachelle, the aunt and uncle who raised her, my wife. We never told our children."

"Did you know about Henri's seizures?"

Hubert sighed. "Yes. He was staying here when he had the first, about sixteen months ago. He insisted on seeing a doctor who would keep his condition confidential. I asked him about it in November. Once he started the medication, he had no further seizures."

"Did anyone else know about them?"

"The doctor, who also saw him in November. And, again, my wife."

"Okay. That's all the questions I have for now. I'll call you if I think of anything else."

"Thank you, Chief. I am grateful that my brother has a friend who is also a skilled detective. You will get justice for Henri."

Chapter 8

Jared returned to Tranquility grateful that Hiro had not consumed any of Henri's wine.

Lars met him in the shuttle bay. "Dr. Klein already has one person in the infirmary for testing."

"Who?"

"Gordon Sheldon."

"Gordon? I didn't know he and Henri were friends."

"Ya. Gordon has been taking his Healthy Living classes to the farm and had Henri talk to them about nutrition. At Christmastime, Henri gave him a pouch of his best wine. That is all I know."

Jared finished strapping on his weights. "Let's go."

They jogged through the tunnel and pod, right to the infirmary waiting room. The man on duty at the reception desk motioned for them to follow.

Dr. Klein saw them coming and jerked his head toward his office. They waited till the door closed. "He has traces of the compound in his blood, at far lower levels than Henri. He has experienced fatigue. His O2 concentration is on the low side of normal. We are administering oxygen to see if it improves."

"And, if it doesn't?" Jared asked.

"I think, because he only ingested one glass, we have some time. Multiple labs are working to develop an antidote."

"Did he tell you when he drank the wine?"

"New Year's Eve."

"And it's stayed in his system for *three months*. Henri drank two glasses of wine every day. How did he survive this long?"

"He seems to have brought the tainted wine back in November. We did an inventory. I think he used up his old stock first. We only found two unpoisoned pouches. Both were rare, expensive wines. Based on his consumption rate, I think he started regularly drinking the tainted wine about a month ago."

"Will Gordon be okay?"

Dr. Klein's computer spoke. "Nurse Phillips requests admission."

"We'll find out now. Enter." The nurse handed Klein a tablet. He scrolled through the information. "Keep him at this level for two hours and check again. If the O2 still looks good, discontinue the oxygen for an hour and run another check. Keep me informed."

Jared did not wait for the door to close behind her. "He's responding to treatment?"

"His O2 level is much more acceptable. But I believe that, without supplemental oxygen, it will drop again. I think he will need oxygen until we find an antidote."

"Will you send him back to Earth?"

"Not advisable, or necessary. I wouldn't want him on a ten-hour flight without access to medical facilities. And an oxygen generator is very easy to carry. Once we determine the therapeutic level, he should be able to resume his usual activities."

Jared raised his eyebrows. "You're pushing the envelope, Doc."

"It's time Earth realizes that we are more than capable of treating many conditions here. There is no reason for expectant mothers to be banished after their sixth month. We are perfectly capable of delivering babies. People with a well-managed seizure disorder, like Henri, shouldn't have to keep it a secret to work here." He pinched the bridge of his nose. "I'm sorry for the rant. Sometimes I feel like an ugly step-child."

"I hear you. Can we talk to Gordon?"

"Yes. He's anxious. See if you can reassure him."

They left the office and Klein told another nurse to show them to Gordon's room.

When the teacher saw Jared and Lars, he forced a smile. "G'day, officers. Would you tell me what the bloody hell is going on? Did Henri have some bad wine?"

Jared shook his hand. "First, remember that you had one glass and Henri drank one or two a day. Okay?"

"Right. So you're saying that I'm not about to keel over."

"Right. Henri was murdered. The wine was poisoned."

"Bloody hell. Who would kill Henri? He wouldn't hurt a fly."

"That's what we're trying to figure out. We think it may be related to something that happened decades ago."

"What was in the stuff? Do they have to ship the antidote from Earth?"

"Something new. They're working on an antidote. In the meantime, Doc says that the oxygen is controlling your symptoms. Are you feeling better?"

"Quite a bit." Gordon paused. "There's no antidote?"

"No known antidote. Several labs have its chemical composition. It shouldn't take them long to come up with one."

"What would have happened if you hadn't issued that bulletin?"

"I don't know. Has the fatigue worsened in the past weeks?"

"I don't believe so. Some days are better than others. It's been going on three months now. I was sort of getting used to feeling tired all the time. I had a checkup the end of January. They didn't find anything."

"Henri had his physical a month ago. That wouldn't include the full blood panel you had today, but they should have tested your oxygen level."

"They did."

"You get some rest. I'll see what Doc has to say about that. But remember that we're working the case."

"Catch the bastard. Henri was a good bloke."

"We will." Jared led the way back to Klein's office. The door stood open. "Got a minute?"

Klein motioned them in. "Questions?"

"One. When Gordon had his checkup in January and Henri had his physical last month, what was their blood oxygen level?"

"Low normal." Klein shook his head. "I've been kicking myself about that. But Henri denied any fatigue. Gordon *was* complaining about fatigue. I suggested some ways to improve the oxygen level and told him to come back in a month if symptoms persisted. He didn't. I read him the riot act today."

"You probably see people with low normals on a regular basis who live for years."

"Not so much here. But on Earth I did."

"Hindsight is twenty-twenty. Keep me posted.

***

By the time Jared got home that afternoon, Karen was already there.

When he walked in, she hugged him. "How are you doing?"

"Okay. We're making some progress. If we get stalled, it will really hit me."

"The whole place is buzzing. People kept asking me if it's true that Henri was murdered. I gave my standard answer. Even if I knew anything, I couldn't say."

"They'll stop asking after the evening news. I went to Regina before she could hunt me down for an interview. I didn't want people to panic, thinking there was a killer on the loose."

"There isn't?"

"Henri brought the poisoned wine with him from Earth. Video from his apartment shows no evidence that anyone tampered with it here."

"Who would want to kill Henri?"

"It's somehow related to events decades ago. Have you ever heard of the *Cause Vertueuse?*"

"Maybe." She pursed her lips. "Was it an extremist group?"

"Yeah. I hope the community doesn't have to hear this. Henri fell in love with the leader's daughter, married her, had a daughter of his own, then his conscience forced him to leave them both behind."

"Oh-h. That explains a lot. I wish he had felt safe enough to tell us about his daughter."

Jared smiled without humor. "He knew me too well. He knew I would ask a lot of questions about why he abandoned his family. Questions he couldn't afford to answer. He told me everything in his will."

"I'm glad he did. Does it help?"

"Yeah. It would have hurt to learn all this from someone else. And not knowing would have really derailed our investigation. I would have been banging my head against the wall trying to figure out a motive."

"You need to unwind. Why don't you hop in the turbo-shower. I got a pizza. I didn't think you'd want to go out tonight."

"Thanks. I'll be right back."

***

"Good morning, Chief." When Rita's voice came over the apartment's speakers while he was still dressing, Jared grabbed his earpiece.

"Report."

She spoke into his ear. "You have an incoming call from Captain Julian in Paris."

"Give me a minute to get to the camera." He shrugged on his vest and closed it while walking to the kitchen. He kissed Karen.

She raised her eyebrows. "Development?"

"Call from Earth. Stay out of sight." He sat in front of the video phone. "Rita, connect call."

Captain Julian appeared on the screen. "Bon jour, Chief. Did I wake you?"

"No. I was getting ready for work. Do you have new information?"

"We found the compound in Dubois's samples. He *was* poisoned. We are reopening the other three cases."

"Any evidence that he was a CV member?"

"I spoke to his wife this morning. She was reluctant. But when I stressed to her that he may have been murdered because of his past, she admitted it. He told her before they married."

"Did she know of any other CV members?"

"She remembered one, twenty years ago, so she could not give a description. Her husband explained that former members make a practice of not speaking to one another unless they are alone. In this case, she and Dubois were in a market, shopping separately. She saw the interaction. Her husband quickly sent the man on his way. When she asked, he told her how he knew the man."

Jared shook his head. "Protecting former members will get them all killed. Rachelle Le Claire wouldn't give me names either. Although I'm hoping she'll at least tell me the name of the one Henri saw while he was there. I'm giving her time to think about it."

"She was also uncooperative with me. She refused protection, believing she is in no danger. We are monitoring cameras near her home. I told her to contact me if she experiences any unusual fatigue."

"Are you testing Mrs. Dubois?"

"Today. However, her fatigue seems more from the stress of her husband's death."

"Henri lived alone and he liked wine. It was relatively easy to poison him without harming anyone else. Dubois would have been more difficult."

"Indeed. I will have investigators ask family members of other potential victims if they are experiencing fatigue symptoms."

"Good call, Captain."

"I feel like this case is bringing us closer to friendship. Please, call me Renee."

"Renee, I'm Jared. But everybody except my wife calls me Chief."

Renee chuckled. "What my husband calls me, I cannot repeat in public. I will inform you of any further developments. Au revoir, Chief."

"Thanks, Renee. Rita, end call."

Karen brought his coffee, smiling. "First name basis. Getting chummy with the female captain."

"We've known each other for three years. We have a pretty good rapport. It was time."

"At least she's thousands of miles away. Unlike Halolani."

"Hey!"

"I've seen you leering at her." She smiled.

He stood and kissed her. "I'm not leering. Just admiring." He wrapped his arm around her waist. "I have all I can handle right here."

"And don't you forget it. Now, go put your pants on."

Chapter 9

The next morning, during Jared's rounds, many people thanked him for doing the interview to stop the rumor mill. He patrolled with his fourth Tranquility officer, Rudy Rodriguez, for a few minutes before heading to his office.

He had almost reached it when Rita's voice came again. "Incoming call from the North Pole infirmary."

"Go ahead."

"Chief, this is Dr. Smirnov at North Pole."

"Good morning, doctor. Do you have someone showing symptoms?"

"Two. Jamie and Nick Roberts."

"She's the farm manager, right?" Jared entered the office.

"Yes. Henri Le Claire gave them wine for Christmas. They saved it until their anniversary on February 14th."

"Have you talked to Dr. Klein about a course of treatment?"

"Yes. We had already administered oxygen. We are running the same O2 level tests."

"How much wine did they consume?"

"One glass each."

"Did you and Dr. Klein compare levels of the compound in their systems to his patient?"

"We did. The two men were about the same. Jamie's is marginally less. We thought exactly what you're thinking. Once it's in the bloodstream, it does not dissipate. Is it less toxic to women? Was absorption effected by the amount of food in her stomach? I questioned her. They *both* drank the entire glass. We don't have enough victims to reach a conclusion."

"There may be more on Earth." Jared settled into his chair. "I hope anyone who drank Henri's wine here would have already reported to their clinic."

"Nick works the night shift. Jamie waited for him to get off work before they came in. I told her how foolish that was."

"I didn't want to create a panic with my bulletin. I probably didn't convey enough urgency."

"I understand. I will relay any further developments to Dr. Klein."

"Thanks, doctor. Rita, end call." He drummed his fingers on the desk for a moment. "Rita, what's on my schedule today?"

"At 1500, you are scheduled as guest instructor for the fifth and sixth grade martial arts class."

Jared smiled. It would be a nice break from the current investigation. "What about next week?"

"On Monday, you have a lunch appointment with Marguerite Boyle. On Tuesday you are scheduled to begin visits to the other bases. And next Friday, the flight from Mars is expected to land at Armstrong base. You are one of the dignitaries who will greet them."

"I don't feel like much of a dignitary. I can meet with base security while I'm there. And I just got back from Taurus. We can eliminate those two from my regular stops. When the time comes, I plan to escort Henri's body to Apennine. That takes care of them. I'll probably delay the trip to North Pole, depending on this case. Alert my staff there that the situation is fluid."

"Message sent. Incoming call from Captain Julian."

"Put her through." He waited for Renee's image to appear. "You have another development."

"Oi. Mrs. Dubois had no trace of the compound. However, Mr. Dubois kept a favorite snack food in his desk at work. She said that he only ate it there. We were able to test what remained. All contained the poison."

"You'll want to see if he shared any with his co-workers and have them tested. A single glass of Henri's wine has left three of our people with symptoms."

Renee swore. "Pardon me. You have lost more people?"

"No. Just fatigue which responds to supplemental oxygen. In low doses, it's treatable. However, it does not seem to dissipate. Men who consumed the same amount forty-five days apart have the same level."

"The sooner someone develops an antidote, the better. One moment." She waved someone in, then reached up and took a tablet. She nodded and gave orders in French. "Some of the results I was waiting for. Two more of the deaths can be attributed to the poison. And we have another victim. The Swiss man's wife succumbed last night, despite valiant attempts to save her."

Jared leaned back. "So our killer is trying not to harm others, but he's willing to risk collateral damage."

"Yes. Our killer also has resources."

"Scary resources. He poisoned *only* Henri's wine and *only* Dubois's snacks. He has to be highly intelligent."

"Why now, after decades?"

"Maybe he didn't have the resources before." Jared shrugged. "Maybe it didn't matter before. If he was about to do something that would put his face in public view . . ."

"Such as running for a political office."

"Possibly."

"This assumes that the killer is a former CV member. Have you rejected the idea that it is someone seeking revenge?"

"I haven't rejected it. But there's a problem with that theory. How did the killer get the names of CV members who were unknown to law enforcement?"

"Ah-h, yes. The killer would need a former CV accomplice."

"So, even if the killer is out for revenge, we need to find the former CV member who gave him the names. Either way, we need the names of former members."

"We will interview our list of known members. They have no love for law enforcement. However, they could also be in danger.

Maybe that will loosen their tongues. Please speak to Rachelle Le Claire again. Oh, you were on the morning news."

"I was?" He sighed. "Of course. Our news anchor wants to move on to bigger and better things. Her job here is mostly fluff."

"She fed the story to the news services. It may be to our advantage. I will ask my supervisor for permission to hold a media briefing. That may also motivate former CV members to cooperate."

"If Rachelle has returned to work, I'll wait till this evening to talk to her."

"Very well. I will speak to you again tomorrow."

***

That evening, Rachelle again declined to give him names, but said that she would speak to the members she knew. Jared thanked her, but urged caution.

He checked news from France and found stories concerning the poisonings.

The next morning, Renee called while he walked to his office. "Go ahead, Renee. I don't have video right now."

"I am afraid that we have an explosion of cases in Europe. We have two in critical condition, another death, and nine people with treatable symptoms."

"Results from the press conference?"

"For the most part. When I tried to contact a woman on the list of former members, she had died on Wednesday. Her husband was ill. He is one of the critical cases. One of the treatable cases was a co-worker of Dubois."

"I need the treating facilities to share information with Dr. Klein here at Tranquility. He has point on the medical end of this. He's trying to determine if this stuff ever dissipates or if it just continues to accumulate till it's effects are irreversible." Jared entered his office and Renee's image appeared on the wall.

"It will be done. Oh, the forth person you found was also a victim of the poison."

"Rita found it, not me."

"Of course. I cannot imagine doing police work without my computer. We are working closely with French and Swiss authorities. I will talk to more known CV members today."

"I guess we're at a standstill till one of them talks."

"I am afraid so." She shook her head. "There is only a slender chance that one of them is the killer. We already tore apart their pasts. They can never be taken off the restricted list. However, they could be the name source for a revenge killer."

"True. You still have leads to follow. I'm stalled here." He sighed. "It's frustrating."

"I understand. I have been in your position. Stay in friendly contact with Rachelle Le Claire. There must be a memorial service for her father. And arrangements for transport of his body back to Earth. You have excuses to contact her."

"I'll do that."

"And I will contact you daily. More often if there are significant developments."

"Thanks, Renee. Rita, end call. Might as well get back to my routine. Show me the new arrivals." He studied the Lunar Adventures passenger manifest for a moment. *Only eleven this time.* "Let's see the bios on those headed for Tranquility."

Rita displayed four newcomers scheduled to work at Tranquility and one child. The first was a big wig. Sequent Mining's new chief of operations. *That will take some getting used to. I have Karl pretty well-trained.* He smiled. *I'll have to tell him that.*

A couple with a seven-year-old daughter were both chef's. She would be working in the fine-dining restaurant while he took charge of the school cafeteria.

The fifth newcomer was a graduate student from the University of Arizona School of Geology. She would be on a work study program for the next year. Lunar graduate students usually worked in housekeeping, custodial service, or day care. They had to earn their room and board.

"Rita, schedule lunch appointments with the new residents the week after they get to Tranquility."

"I will make the arrangements."

***

After Renee's call on Monday reporting no progress, Jared needed a distraction, like lunch with Marguerite Boyle. When he entered the corporate cafeteria, he barely recognized her.

"Your picture doesn't do you justice."

She blushed. "You know how those ID photos are. Plus, I treated myself while I was in quarantine. I changed my hair and had my eyebrows done."

"That's a good way to kill time during quarantine." He gestured to a table and they took seats. "But I'm going to ask you to get a new ID photo."

"I understand. I will get that done later today."

"Do you have any questions for me?"

"I will admit that I was somewhat nervous when your computer called to schedule this lunch. Until everyone assured me that you have lunch with all new residents."

"Sort of welcome to the neighborhood. Have you ever lived in a small town?"

"I have not."

"Well, you are now living in a small town. Everyone knows everyone. Other than the low gravity, it's probably the biggest adjustment to living here. People find common ground. Any New Englander will go out of their way to meet you. Someone from Newfoundland will consider you a neighbor."

"Oh." She picked up her sandwich. "They should tell us this during orientation. I was somewhat taken aback by how friendly one of my co-workers has been. She is from Boston."

Jared chuckled. "I'll make that suggestion to HR. Are you wondering about anything else?"

"I have noticed a few people wearing vests that reach to below their knees. The garments look very awkward."

"Earth vests. Extra weight. Those people are planning a trip back to Earth soon. It reduces the time it takes to adjust to Earth's gravity. Most people wear weighted garments all the time. To help maintain muscle mass." He tapped his vest. "This isn't bulletproof."

"Oh, of course. I never considered that you wouldn't need one here." She hesitated. "Everyone is talking about the murder."

"They told you that his wine was poisoned on Earth."

"Yes."

"So there's nothing to worry about. I'm working on the case with authorities there."

"You must be a very good investigator."

"And you must be very good at your job. We all are."

"Ah, yes. Only the best work here."

***

That Friday, Jared turned his spacesuit over to the ground crew and headed for the passenger lounge. He would enjoy this shuttle flight more than the last one.

He liked shuttle flights. One hour in a shuttle without a suit as opposed to a six-hour rover drive unable to scratch his nose. *What's not to like?*

He found the other dignitaries had arrived ahead of him. Today's passengers included Karl Schultz, Sequent Mining's outgoing chief-of-operations, Tranquility mayor Angela Carlson, also the school principal, and their spouses.

Everyone knew everyone in the settlement, so there was no shortage of conversation. For a while, they grilled Jared about the murder investigation.

He answered a few questions, then sighed. "I hope you'll understand. I'd like to try to take my mind off Henri's murder for awhile. Can we change the subject?"

After a short silence, Angela glanced around the room. "Chief, where's Karen today?"

"Karl's such a slave driver she couldn't get the day off." Jared smiled.

Karl shook his finger. "I asked her twice if she wanted to go."

"He's right, Angela. She attended the first landing and the first send off. Since then, she's preferred to stay home and work."

Angela shrugged. "I can't imagine not wanting to take a shuttle. This is not only our first shuttle flight, but our first visit to Armstrong. We've taken rover trips to the other bases when the teams played."

"I'll bet you just ran for mayor for the perks."

"They kind of make up for the headaches. I suppose you'll forego the base tour."

"Yeah. I'm there once a month. It's a lot smaller than the other bases, so I know it better than North Pole, Taurus or Apennine. I'll meet with the security team while I'm there."

"But you'll join us at the luncheon."

"Of course. I have to eat."

Angela fidgeted in her seat for a moment. "I can't imagine going to Mars. Being forty days from Earth if there was an emergency."

"That's why only astronauts are stationed there yet. It takes a special kind of person. If Karen had wanted to go there, we would've had a problem."

Karl huffed. "It still took us two years to get her here."

"You even created a job for me to make it happen." Jared flashed a grin.

"That is not *entirely* true. The Lunar Governing Board had discussed a police force when we agreed on the law code. And the old security guards didn't have enough training. When I learned of your background, it motivated me to push the idea."

Angela looked from one to the other. "That's why we have Lunar Enforcement? I never knew. Karl, it was a stellar idea. The LE officers are so much more professional than the old security guards. I saw the guards break up a drunken brawl once. I've heard that the LE officers do it just by showing up."

"Public relations," Jared said. "When new employees arrive, they see a video of the demonstrations we put on after I started. Great deterrent."

"I'll say. It made me want to stay out of trouble."

Jared chuckled. "By the way, Karl, is this your last formal function?"

"Other than my retirement party, yes. But that is two months off yet. Desjarlais will need some training."

"He's been with Sequent Mining a long time?"

"Almost two decades. He's been head of our Canadian division for the past four years."

"I have you pretty well-trained. I hope he's as easy to get along with."

"Like you said, he'll see the video." This time, Karl grinned. "I've only been easy to get along with because, as Angela said, your people scare me."

Everyone laughed.

Chapter 10

On Monday, Renee again had no progress to report. Jared acted professional until the call ended, even though he felt like punching something. He patrolled alone in the most isolated parts of the settlement, hoping no one would talk to him.

At 11:30, Rita reminded him of his lunch appointment with Anita Douglas. *Time to stop being anti-social. Maybe this will help take my mind off the case.*

At the cafeteria, he followed the graduate student, almost as tall as him, to a table. "You've probably met my wife already."

Anita nodded. "Dr. Mason-Pearce said to expect this invitation."

"Did *she* tell you anything about us?"

"She was pretty busy. She said your kids are about my age. Otherwise, all I know about you is what I saw in the orientation video. It was pretty intimidating."

"Good. We want new people to know that they aren't dealing with poorly-trained security guards. I hired only experienced officers who were ready to slow down. Eleven of them had retired after twenty years at their previous job."

"But the ones I've seen aren't old."

"Most cops start in their early twenties. They can retire in their forties and start a new career. I'm second-oldest in my department."

"Why'd you decide to become a cop?"

"I like investigating. I joined the Navy and chose Shore Patrol as my specialty. When my hitch was almost up, an NCIS special agent recruited me." He smiled. "The rest is history."

"Where are you from?"

"We're both originally from Minnesota. Because of my career, we've lived all over the world. Now we have a little hobby ranch near Santa Fe."

"I'm from *Gallup.*"

"I know." Jared smiled. "I read your personnel file."

"Can I ask a stupid question?"

"Go ahead."

"How do they play soccer here without the ball hitting the dome every time they kick it?"

Jared chuckled. "I believe the balls were designed by an engineer and a physicist. They're much heavier then the soccer balls used on Earth. They mimic how the ball would behave there. They were able to do the same with the racquet balls and handballs so the skills people learned there transfer here. They haven't perfected basketballs yet. You can shoot baskets here, but you can't dribble." Rita's voice came in his ear. "Excuse me. Go ahead, Rita."

"Dr. Klein asked if you would stop by his office after lunch."

"Tell him I'll be there in about twenty minutes. Thanks, Rita. So, Anita, why did you choose geology?"

"I spent a lot of time hiking the mesas and canyons around Gallup. But, to be honest, I thought that of all the things I found interesting, geology was the quickest way to get here." She got a far-off look. "I remember when this base was founded. I thought working here would be stellar. Being accepted for the work study program is beyond my wildest dreams."

"Good. I'll bet you haven't experienced any low-grav sickness."

"None. After weightlessness, this is great. How long have you wanted to come to the moon?"

"I'll let you know when it happens." He laughed at her confusion. "I'm here because of Karen. And I'll be here as long as she wants to be here."

***

"Give me some good news, Doc," Jared said, standing in Klein's doorway.

"I released Gordon today with supplemental oxygen to use when he's up and active. The same is true of Jamie and Nick Roberts."

"That's great news." He sank into a chair. "But that's not why you called me here."

"I've studied the non-fatal cases. We still don't have enough to reach scientific conclusions, but I have a few educated guesses. I've bounced them off my counterparts in Europe and they concur."

"Any good news there?"

"A glimmer of hope, even without an antidote. The oldest known date of ingestion is approximately eight months ago. The poison *is* slowly flushed out of the system. That victim's level is about half that of Gordon and Nick. Women who have ingested the poison all seem to have a lower level than men."

"As long as these people don't ingest more poison, they'll get better?"

"We believe so."

"That's really great. Have there been any more deaths on Earth?"

"No. The two critical cases are stable for now. Fortunately, their bodies were still able to respond to high levels of oxygen. Doctors are trying blood transfusions. It could work."

"Let's hope so."

"When is Henri's memorial service?"

"Saturday. I'm escorting his body to Apennine on Tuesday. His funeral will be Friday in France. I'm supposed to speak by video."

"Do you speak French?"

"I can say 'You're under arrest' in nine languages." He flashed a crooked smile. "The French phrases I know would be useless in a eulogy. Good thing ninety percent of the people on the planet learn English as a second language."

"You should at least learn a couple of phrases before then. At least a quote from scripture."

"Good idea. Henri was a devout man. It would be a nice way to end my eulogy."

Chapter 11

Jared met Lloyd Desjarlais for lunch in a private room in the corporate cafeteria.

Desjarlais shook his hand, but looked annoyed. "Karl tells me that lunch with the police chief is a rite of passage here."

"I like to get to know all my new residents. Lunch is my way of keeping it informal."

"It is the first thing that he has sent me off to do alone. Karl says that you are the most respected man lunar-wide."

"That's nice of him. If I am, it's because I travel to all the settlements more often than most. People have at least met me."

For the first time, Desjarlais smiled. "That is even greater testimony. They have met you and still respect you. I read your file, as I'm sure you read mine. We almost grew up neighbors."

"You're right. By today's standards, Ontario and Minnesota aren't that far apart. I joined the Navy to get out of the cold, but you ended up in the Yukon."

"Only because it was a promotion. When this position became available, I decided that it would be a good place to finish my career. The perfect climate."

Jared chuckled. "That's true. Will your wife be joining you?"

"In a month or two. She is thawing out at our vacation home in New Orleans. I think that when the heat and humidity become oppressive, she will make the trip. I expect that she will continue to spend summers here and winters there."

"I'm looking forward to meeting her." He ate for a moment. "Do you have any questions for me?"

"Karl thought it was important to talk about you and your job." He drank coffee. "He warned me not to let the fact that I am one of your bosses go to my head."

"That's good advice. I, and my officers, will give you the respect your position deserves. But if you mess up, you'll get the same treatment a custodian would. Just ask the former COO of Aqua Luna."

"Karl specifically showed me the news stories about that incident. It is good to know that we have an effective police force. Especially with recent news. He said the man brought the poisoned products with him from Earth?"

"Yes. So there's nothing to worry about."

"Good." Desjarlais finished his grilled chicken. "I saw on the news that there are other victims in Europe."

"Unfortunately, yes."

"Have you turned the investigation over to authorities there?"

"No. I'm working with Interpol."

"Well." He leaned back. "I am not easily impressed. You just succeeded."

Jared smiled with one corner of his mouth. "After thirty years in law enforcement, about half of it outside the United States, I've worked with Interpol a few times. It's just part of the job. But, if I impressed you, I probably don't have to worry about you causing problems. So that's good."

Desjarlais laughed. "No need to worry. I have never been considered a troublemaker and do not intend to start now."

"Then we'll get along just fine."

***

Jared stood still while members of the ground crew strapped him into his spacesuit. Henri's coffin, just a sealed rectangular container, had already been secured on the rover, along with other cargo.

The rover bus had a full load today, twelve passengers. Six were headed back to Earth, two on vacation, the other four permanently. Three had relatives visiting and would spend the time talking to them through glass. Two others, like Jared, had business at Apennine. He planned to stay overnight and consult with his officers there.

The ground crew chief fastened Jared's clear helmet before speaking. "Communications check."

"Loud and clear."

"You're good to go, Chief. Proceed to the airlock."

Jared grinned. "Thanks, Chief." They had the same exchange every time he took a rover trip. He joined the others already there.

"I won't miss this," a woman said.

"Amen." The man beside her nodded inside his helmet.

"It's probably my least favorite part of living here," Jared agreed. "But I try to keep it in perspective. A century ago, the suits the Apollo astronauts wore were about twice as bulky."

The woman chuckled. "Chief, has anyone ever told you that you're an optimist?"

"Life is full of choices. I can choose to be miserable by dwelling on the negative things, or not. Space suits are just an inconvenience."

The crew chief followed the last passenger to the airlock door. "Okay, folks, we're ready to depressurize. Have a safe trip."

He closed the inside door. Two minutes later, the outside door opened and external crew members helped them into the bus, with its four rows of three seats, plus one for the driver, and room in the back for cargo and luggage. It had a roof—but only to provide space for solar panels—and open sides. With all passengers seated, a padded safety bar extended toward them like some amusement park ride.

The driver followed the well-worn trail away from the settlement, staying under the thirty kilometer per hour posted speed limit. The rovers kicked up dust. With no wind, it settled close to its point of origin. Slow speeds kept it from settling on the clear settlement domes.

Lunar Enforcement did issue an occasional speeding ticket, usually to someone new to lunar driving. His lieutenants at each settlement checked the computer logs of all vehicles weekly. If one was speeding in an area with posted limits, the driver of record received a citation. Penalties only involved a small fine and community service, but three speeding tickets earned you a one-way trip back to Earth. No one had ever gotten their second.

The rover passed over a hump protecting fiber optic cable which brought sunlight to the settlement during the two-week night. Solar collectors lay hundreds of kilometers east and west of Tranquility, Taurus, Apennine, and Armstrong base, because plants produced better under natural light. North Pole experienced almost constant daylight.

Leaving Tranquility behind, the driver accelerated to top speed, eighty kph. The trip to Apennine would take about eight hours.

Jared watched the landscape. *I really like shuttles.*

Some passengers chatted. Jared pushed the mute button on his suit, allowing him to hear only what the driver might say.

"Rita, call Ty."

"Calling Lieutenant Collinsworth."

"Mornin', Chief. Y'all on your way?"

"Yeah. I'll get there eventually. Give me a report."

"Well, those of us on the dark side have had to deal with more than our share of drunken tourists with Mardi Gras and all."

Jared chuckled. Only one of his Apennine officers worked on the employee side of the base. The rest worked with the tourists, what they called the dark side. "Did you have to lock up anyone?"

"One guy, overnight. When he sobered up a little we reminded him that the paper he signed didn't say what kind of room and meals Lunar Adventures had to provide him. He saw the light."

"Good. Today's the last day, isn't it?"

"Fat Tuesday. Can I get a Hallelujah?"

Jared laughed. "Hallelujah. Thanks, Ty. I needed a little comic relief."

"So, when do I get to come over from the dark side?"

"Lars is planning to retire in six months. After you go through quarantine, I'm transferring you to Tranquility."

Ty's whistle hurt Jared's ear. "Hallelujah! Wait till I tell the little woman."

"Any news on the baby front?"

"He's moving into place. I'll be headin' out on the next ship."

"Good thing he waited till after Mardi Gras."

"I told Jenny she'd better hold off. The chief wouldn't appreciate losing me during one of our busiest times of year."

"At least when one of you on the dark side needs time off on short notice, I can get a temp in a couple of days. You've made arrangements with Lunar Adventures."

"Their security guy will be on the ship that's taking me back to Texas. Course, he wasn't a Ranger, but he was an MP for twenty years. He'll do okay."

"We'll muddle through. Anything else to report?"

"Folks were a little uneasy when they heard about the murder. Lunar Adventures quit serving wine till I told them which wineries the poison came from. They didn't have many, but they gave it all to me for testing. All negative, but Lunar Adventures didn't want them back. What should I do with them?"

"Give them to deserving employees. After you tell them the whole story."

"Not cops."

"No. We don't want it to look like we're taking advantage of our office."

"Got it. I'd rather drink beer anyhow. I've made reservations for all of us to have dinner at *The Round Table* tonight."

"Thanks. Since It's the best way for me to visit with you guys. Tomorrow morning, I'll put on an isolation suit and patrol with whoever's on duty. I'd better let you get back to work. I'll talk to you more when I get there."

"Phyllis will meet you at the airlock. See y'all later."

***

Jared spent most of the rest of his trip making calls or talking with Rita. Though the helmet had a heads-up display, the person sitting next to him could also see it. He could not view sensitive evidence.

The rover entered a mountain pass where lunar heavy equipment had been used to clear the trail in places. A person could drop a leg into the holes left by the long spikes used to give the "earth-movers" traction.

On the other side of the pass, the driver stopped to let his passengers enjoy the view. Rover bus drivers always did. Everyone looked out on a forty kilometer wide, open-ended valley with Apennine on the far slope.

A few kilometers ahead, Jared saw a tourist rover climbing the mountain. His rover bus would get off the one-way trail long before they met. But they would still have to stop to visit for a few minutes. The tourists had little chance to talk to locals, other than those who worked for Lunar Adventures.

This stop took longer because of the full bus. The employees had to introduce themselves, including their job, reason for this trip, and hometown. If one of the tourists hailed from nearby, excited chatter ensued. They took a lot of pictures with their helmet-cams before the rovers moved on.

As usual, Jared could not wait for the trip to end. He entered the airlock and stood by the inside door. Once he left the airlock, his rank got him out of his space suit first.

"Thanks, everyone." He entered the men's changing room, grabbed his bags and cleaned up before going out to meet Sergeant Phyllis Howard.

"Good afternoon, Chief. Sorry for your loss."

"Thanks, Phyllis. Are all the arrangements in order for the transport of Henri's body?"

"Yes, sir. The ship will be here tomorrow and leave Thursday morning. Another ship will take him from Spaceport Shepard to Paris."

"Good."

"Are you ready to stretch your legs?" She started walking without waiting for a reply.

"Let's drop this stuff at my room, then patrol the light side."

"Only the best come over to the light side. Nothing exciting ever happens here."

"That's why I picked someone with public information experience for this job."

Phyllis shrugged. "I'm not complaining. But once in awhile, when the guys have been dealing with rowdy tourists, I get a little jealous. Then I remember that I never have to work nights."

"Good attitude. You meet just as many interesting people over here."

***

Jared and his officers ate dinner at Apennine's unique, long, narrow restaurant. A clear wall divided all of the round tables in half. It had one kitchen, on the light side, but wait staff on either side, allowing employees to enjoy a meal with visiting family and friends without fear of catching a bug.

It was also the perfect way for Jared to visit with his four officers on the dark side.

As usual, Jared steered the conversation toward home and family until after they placed their orders. When the waiters departed, the officers talked shop. Finally, the topic turned to Henri's murder. Jared answered all of their questions, omitting any mention of the CV.

But they had heard news from Earth. Phyllis cleared her throat. "I've heard that most of the victims had been members of the *Cause Vertueuse*. I can't believe I'm even asking this. Was Henri?"

Jared took in a deep breath, then let it out. "He left ten years before the crackdown because of a crisis of conscience. He only joined because he fell in love with the leader's daughter."

"Oh-h. I just couldn't wrap my mind around Henri—probably the nicest person I have ever met—as a member of an extremist group."

Ty shrugged. "I don't know about y'all, but I sure did something stupid over a girl when I was a youngster."

"I got benched," Jared said. "I was letting Karen tackle me way too often in practice."

That produced a chuckle, then Ty asked what had been in the back of Jared's mind since the day of Henri's murder.

"Have y'all considered the daughter as a suspect? Her daddy deserted her. And that means she stayed with the CV. That could really mess with a kid's head."

"I haven't wanted to." Jared let his breath out. "But I have. If she's a sociopath, she could fake the grief I've seen. She could have faked her happy reunion with Henri. She would be capable of this elaborate plot. She also has a PhD in chemistry and works in medical research. She has the skills to create a poison. I don't believe it, but that doesn't mean I'm ignoring it."

"The girl could have gotten indoctrinated into the gang's ideology," Phyllis said.

"I've considered that. Captain Julian of Interpol is quietly investigating Henri's daughter, letting me stay the supportive friend."

"You're the good cop to her bad cop."

Jared shrugged. "Sort of. Hopefully, Rachelle never finds out about the investigation. And I *really* hope it goes nowhere. I hate to even consider the possibility that Henri's daughter killed him." He sighed, opened his mouth to say more, then closed it.

Phyllis patted his back. "Hang in there, Chief. You lost your best friend."

"Hell, yeah," Ty said. "Y'all rolled up your sleeves and waded into the investigation. And Interpol didn't take over the case. They're working with y'all. Always professional. Give yourself a break, Chief."

The other officers voiced their agreement.

Jared nodded. "Thanks, guys. I've been compartmentalizing. Friday and Saturday, I'll give myself time to grieve."

Chapter 12

On Friday, Jared wore his dress uniform to deliver Henri's eulogy. About fifty people gathered with him and Karen to watch the service in France. Jared noticed when the camera panned out to show the inside of the church, that roughly the same number of mourners gathered there. Henri had left Earth a decade ago.

Jared also thought he recognized a woman sitting in one of the back pews.

The following day, only the soccer field could hold the crowd who attended the memorial service. Sequent Mining suspended operations for eight hours to allow everyone to be there. Hiro and his family traveled from Taurus along with others from all the settlements, even NASA's.

This gathering was more of a celebration of Henri's life than a funeral. Jared M.C.'d the event with Hiro and Karl as scheduled speakers. Others signed up to recall their memories of Henri. Rachelle would watch by video and address the assembly at the conclusion.

Jared had to stop three times during his presentation to regain his composure. He noticed similar pauses from Hiro.

Karl managed to stay businesslike. "Friends and associates, I was on the committee that hired Henri as the first lunar farmer. NASA had experimented with growing plants on the moon, so we already had a little knowledge. But there was much more to learn.

"Henri was *so* enthusiastic. The other candidates talked about 'looking forward to the challenge' and 'the opportunity to make history.' It became apparent to the entire committee that Henri had been *preparing* for the job for a decade. He could recite all the data from the NASA studies. He had even earned himself a spot as an unpaid consultant on those studies. When the committee sat down to make its choice, there was no discussion. We all wanted Henri.

"It was one of the best hires we made. We all eat better today because of Henri. During his tenure, the moon became self-sustaining in the following areas: Vegetables, fruits, eggs, chicken, duck, and catfish. And soon we will have lunar goat cheese. Henri's dream was to make imports of food from Earth unnecessary. Let's keep working toward Henri's dream."

The speech brought shouts, cheers, and whistles.

Then the event returned to a more somber mood as individuals stood to recall their favorite memories of Henri. Even two eighth grade students spoke. They were chosen because they had both lived on the moon since pre-school. They had many memories of Henri and his farm.

Afterward, the cafeteria staff served a lunch made almost entirely of lunar-grown ingredients. People mingled and visited, then began drifting away until only Henri's closest friends and the lunar officers remained.

Jared watched the cafeteria workers collecting their equipment without really seeing them.

"How you doing, boss?" Halolani asked, startling him.

"Okay. Better. I needed this."

"Yeah, you did. You've been working so hard on the investigation, you haven't stepped back."

"I think this will help with the investigation too. I'll be able to focus better."

"Monday."

Jared smiled. "Yes, Monday. I'm taking another day off."

***

Monday morning Jared had a call scheduled with Captain Julian. He settled into his office chair. "Good morning, Renee. Did you see anyone of interest at Henri's funeral?"

"I wondered if you would notice me there."

"I don't often get to see the back of your head. But I recognized the haircut."

She ran her fingers through her close-cropped hair. "I should have worn a hat. I have photographs of all who attended. My computer is reviewing them now. She has already identified three known former CV members. I do not believe that our killer was there."

"There are too many cameras everywhere, which the killer knows we will be monitoring. Any developments?"

She sighed. "I have spoken to *all* the known CV members. Many are afraid and willing to cooperate to an extent. Several even admitted knowing one or more of the deceased."

"So, nothing, then."

She lost her somber face. "I reserved the best for last. I saved a life. While I interviewed a man, I noticed the dark circles under his wife's eyes. She also shuffled when she walked. I asked how long she had been feeling tired."

"Was she a CV member too?"

"She admitted it at the hospital. Tests conducted over the weekend found the poison in a bag of coffee beans. She opened it two weeks ago. Doctors estimate that because of her level of consumption, she would have been dead in another week."

"Her husband doesn't drink coffee?"

"He switched to tea about a month ago."

Jared sat up straighter. "Is he a suspect?"

"We are investigating, but my instincts say no. He seems genuinely distraught. However, until we clear him, he will have no direct access to his wife."

"Good. I guess that gives us another piece of information. Now we know that heat doesn't damage this poison."

"Oui. This is the first case I am aware of where the poison was subjected to heat."

"How many victims do we have who were former CV members and are still capable of answering questions?"

Renee consulted her computer. "Three."

"Ask them if anyone ever questioned their loyalty. Ask this woman's husband too."

"Ah-h. I see. Henri Le Claire left the CV. These other victims survived the crackdown and rejoined society. Someone may see them as traitors."

"Until now, I hadn't considered the possibility that these could be revenge killings by a former CV member."

"It would not have changed the course of our investigation. It is hard to imagine such a zealot surviving to this day. After the crackdown, a few extremists held on, but the governments of the world tracked them down as well."

"I know. Another suspect pool we need to look at is the crackdown children. Someone whose parents may have indoctrinated them at an early age."

"Oui." Renee nodded. "That could explain the delay. The child would have had to wait until he or she had the maturity and resources to exact revenge. Are you certain that you would not like to come here to pursue this case?"

"Yes, I would." Jared hesitated. "I promised Karen when I retired from NCIS that we would never live apart again. That's how I ended up here. But neither of us could have predicted this. All the leads are on Earth. I could be contributing so much more there."

"I can make the arrangements. My superiors would approve."

"Hold off on that." Jared leaned back in his seat. "I need to talk to Karen first. I'll call you tomorrow morning."

***

Jared cooked one of Karen's favorite meals for supper, saying nothing about the idea until after dessert. Still, he hesitated.

Karen watched him over her water glass. "What's on your mind?"

He took a deep breath. "Renee asked me to come to Europe to work the case. I would be more useful there."

"And you told her ... ?"

"I'd have to talk to you first."

Karen's gaze turned icy. "You said we'd never live apart again."

"I know. But who could have predicted this. I'm trying to catch Henri's killer. I won't be gone long."

"How long? Two weeks? A month? Longer? And don't forget the two weeks in quarantine after you get done. Do you think that you can do something that Interpol with all its resources can't do?"

Jared felt his anger rising. Then he saw the tears in her eyes. He hung his head. "Okay."

"W-what?"

He met her gaze again. "You sacrificed enough. Those months at a time alone with three little kids while I was stationed on a carrier. The important events I missed because I got called away on a case. I promised you we would never live apart again and I need to keep my word."

She wiped her eyes and reached out to him. "Thank you."

He took her hand and kissed it. "No, thank you for putting up with this cop all these years. If I get one of these stupid ideas again, you have my permission to whack me on the side of the head."

She tried to smile. "Be careful. I'll do it."

"You'd better."

***

Jared called Renee the next morning. "I'll have to decline the invitation. If we even wrap this case up in a couple weeks—and that's a big if—I'd have to spend another two weeks in quarantine before I could come back. So we'll just have to work together by phone. I owe it to Karen."

"Just as well." She laughed. "Working side-by-side with you would be too distracting."

"Distracting?"

"Mon ami! Have you not noticed that you are a bel homme?"

Jared blushed. "Keep talking like that and I'll tell your husband."

"He is as bad as I. You should hear us when we sit at a sidewalk café, watching passers by."

"You sound like an interesting couple."

"We have been called worse. In regard to the question of loyalty, that is a dead end. I believe the former CV members were honest when they said no one had ever questioned their loyalty. Other than a few zealots, who authorities had to deal with later, they reported that most survivors heard and heeded the message the world sent."

"That was the impression I had. They left the CV behind and became contributing members of society."

"Oi. We *have* had another death. He saw the announcements, but preferred death to standing trial for his roll in the CV. He confessed all in his suicide note."

"Suicide?"

"He recognized the symptoms of the poison and shot himself rather than slowly suffocate. If we had managed to save his life, we simply would have had to execute him later."

"He was *that* bad?"

"He planted several bombs responsible for the deaths of more than twenty people. His confession *may* help us in this case. He believed that the killer is a former CV member and he named names. Fourteen in all. Five that we suspected, but had no proof and nine that had evaded detection. Three of those names are not in the system. The rest we are rounding up today."

"And you saved that for last?" Jared slapped the desk. "Our killer could be among them."

"Correct."

"The three who aren't in the system probably changed their identities."

"And we know how difficult that is."

Jared leaned back. "Anyone in a position of prominence?"

"One small city mayor. Three more in sensitive positions. At the very least, all four will lose their jobs."

"That *could be* a motive. From the beginning, I've wondered about the timing of these murders. Any indication that someone was moving on to bigger and better things?"

"Not yet. I will send you what we have so far on the eleven. Then I will update you as I know more."

"Good. I won't feel so useless. Do you have anything on the three who disappeared?"

"School records. Two enrolled in university before dropping out to join the CV."

"Send me that too."

"Very good. Would you like to see the video of our interviews after we bring them in?"

Jared smiled. "If the interviews are in French, I'm afraid they won't do me much good."

"I will send you the interview for the person living in Britain. And the transcripts of the others. What languages *do* you speak?"

"Spanish, Italian, and broken Japanese. I recognize a few French words, mostly written. Not enough to follow a conversation."

"You are fortunate that English is the universal language. I must prepare for the raids. I will send you the files now. Au revoir."

"Good bye." Jared disconnected and waited a moment.

"Incoming files from Captain Julian," Rita said.

"Open the first in alphabetical order."

Jared studied all eleven files. Other than the four who stood to lose their jobs after their CV membership was exposed, the rest seemed to have no motive for murdering their former compatriots.

He concentrated on those four: the mayor, a court reporter, an assistant to a member of Britain's House of Commons, and a police captain.

He considered the irony that four people who had once been opposed to the government to the point of violence had chosen to go into government service. He felt a little sad too. *It doesn't matter how much good they've done since they left the CV. The laws don't allow forgiveness.*

One after another, all four showed a history of public service starting shortly after the crackdown.

Jean Cartier had gone home to Britain and resumed using his birth name, John Carter. He had enrolled in university there, majoring in political science, graduating with honors. A string of government jobs followed, always with outstanding performance reviews. He had occupied his current position for the past two years. Carter had a wife and two children, was active in his community and church.

"What a waste."

"I did not understand the command, Chief."

"Just talking to myself, Rita. Show me the files on the three who disappeared."

"There is little information."

Rita displayed the first. It included a high school graduation photo and two others of basketball and soccer team members. The girl could best be described as average. She was the same height and build as half her teammates, with the same dark hair and features.

The second CV member had at least enrolled in university, though the file contained nothing more recent than his freshman ID photo. He had a receding hairline, large nose and ears that stuck out.

He would still be easy to spot, if he didn't have cosmetic surgery. A big if.

The third had started her sophomore year of college and probably would still be recognizable, again, without cosmetic surgery. She had blonde hair, but follicles could always be treated to change color.

Jared knew that Interpol would age the pictures and spread them around the world. Every law enforcement agency on the planet would be on the lookout for these three.

"End program." He leaned back and sighed. *I feel so useless here. On Earth, I could be following leads, interviewing suspects. Who may or may not speak English,* he reminded himself.

What would you be doing if you hadn't come here? You might be a city cop, maybe a small town sheriff. You sure wouldn't be working with Interpol on a murder case. Quit feeling sorry for yourself.

He bounded from his chair. "That will be all for now, Rita. I'm going on patrol."

Chapter 13

The next morning, Jared expected a call from Renee. She did not disappoint.

"We arrested all eleven on charges of membership in a terrorist organization. Two seemed relieved. The rest denied the charges. When the nine were informed of the source of our information, six more admitted their CV membership. Three are fighting the allegation."

"Which three?"

"The mayor, court reporter, and a social worker. The police captain said that she would not disrespect her fellow officers by denying the charges. She was one of those who seemed relieved."

"That has to be a terrible burden to carry around all these years." Jared paused. "Will any consideration be given them for what they have contributed to society?"

Renee raised her hands, palms up. "That depends on how deeply they were involved in the CV. If they cannot be connected to any violent crime, several of them may go about their lives. The police captain has twenty years on the force. She may be allowed to retire and collect her pension."

"Maybe I'm just a soft touch. When I read what these people have accomplished since they left the CV, I think of Henri. He was a kind man, good to everyone."

"But remember, Henri Le Claire left the CV due to a crisis of conscience. The eleven we arrested simply escaped the crackdown. They may have changed their ways, or they may have simply been very good at blending in."

"Thanks for reminding me." Jared smiled. "I probably just have too much time to think about it here."

"Put your investigative mind to work on the transcripts of the interviews. Tell me if there are any questions we forgot to ask. I am sending the files now."

He chuckled. "Yes, ma'am."

"And one more thing. The former CV member who switched from coffee to tea has been cleared. He could not have been responsible for any of the killings. He was simply fortunate that he stopped drinking coffee when he did."

"Okay. How is his wife doing?"

"Stable. Responding to treatment."

"Good. The more I thought about it, the less I considered him a viable suspect. I'll talk to you soon." Jared disconnected and started with the police captain's file. The woman had been extremely cooperative.

She had joined the CV right out of high school in 2046, following her boyfriend. She made friends in the group and stayed even after the two broke up. The CV discouraged members from having contact with family outside of the group, but she went home for her sister's wedding.

The crackdown started the next day.

Her family protected her and came up with a story to explain her three-year absence. She entered university, then the police academy. In her twenty years on the force she had anonymously turned in two notorious CV members. She admitted to knowing of three others, like herself, and withholding that information from authorities.

Next, Jared chose the video file containing John Carter's interview. The well-dressed former CV member's posture expressed absolute defeat. Jared could not see the interrogator, male with a British accent.

"When did you join the CV?"

"After I graduated secondary school. I spent the summer touring Europe. I met a French girl at a hostel in Germany. I was smitten by Elaine. We traveled together for a month. At first, I tolerated her politics. Eventually, she won me over. When we returned to the CV compound, my indoctrination really began. She played a big part in that. She ... um ... rewarded me for a job well done."

"What did you do for the cause?"

"My first job was gardening. Growing vegetables, tending the vineyard. Later, they sent me out with Elaine to collect intelligence. We were on one of those missions when the crackdown began."

"What did you do then?"

"I'm afraid I was in shock for a bit." He sighed. "Elaine was outraged. She wanted to get weapons and attack law enforcement facilities. I told her that would be suicide. I convinced her to wait twenty-four hours."

"And?"

"I spent the time trying to convince her that Providence had given us a second chance. We should mend our ways. Elaine would not hear it. She was incensed. I told her that I would not throw my life away for a lost cause. I left. I still had my British passport and used it to go home. Dad and Mum had told everyone that I was traveling about Europe. We simply perpetuated that lie."

"Do you know what happened to Elaine?"

"Three weeks later, she and another CV member attacked an Interpol assault team. Killed two and wounded four more before they were gunned down."

"Have you considered that you may have saved lives if you had turned her in?"

"That thought pricks my conscience from time-to-time. Then I remind myself of my circumstances. I was still in love with her. It broke my heart that she chose a suicide mission over a life with me. I was barely able to decide what to do with myself."

"Do you know of any other former CV members?"

"Of course. All of those you've arrested over the years. Most likely, all that you arrested yesterday. I follow the stories quite closely, hoping to see a friend among those who escaped the crackdown."

"Do you know of any *other* former CV members?"

"I've never seen a former member here in the UK."

Jared sat up straighter, waiting for the interrogator's response. The man moved on to the next question. The rest of the interview provided nothing useful.

"Rita, call Captain Julian."

"Calling Captain Julian."

Jared waited for the connection, but instead of Renee, a younger man appeared on screen.

"My apologees, Chief Pearce, Captain Julian is interviewing a detainee. I am Inspector Gerard. May I assist you?"

"Give her a message. I watched the interrogation of John Carter. When he was asked if he knew of any former CV members, he made a point of replying that he had never seen any *in the UK*. I believe that is significant."

"Thank you, Chief. I will convey the message to her as soon as she is available. She will contact you at the earliest opportunity."

"Thank you. Rita, end call." He stood, paced the two strides across the office, then returned to his desk, but remained standing. "Rita, show me the transcript of the next interview, starting from the beginning of the alphabet."

The first two former CV members had little to lose from discovery. Both had retired. Both had told their spouses about their past. Jared sat for the next transcript.

"Incoming call from Captain Julian."

"Go ahead."

Renee appeared. "Mon ami, I apologize for the delay. I reviewed the section of the interview you referred to. Carter's body language showed no sign of deceit, however, he has practiced lying for so long, that is not surprising. How do you suggest we proceed?"

"Does his job require him to travel outside the UK?"

"Seldom. Several African countries on one trip. The States and Canada on another."

"And on holidays?"

"He traveled extensively. Even to the moon once."

"He won't be traveling anymore. But that won't help us figure out where he saw CV members." Jared leaned back in his chair. "I'd like to have some kind of ammunition before he's questioned again. Something other than accusing him of a half-truth."

"Would you like a copy of his travel history? Perhaps you could find a pattern."

"It will give me something to do once I finish these transcripts. Do you agree that if Carter had contact with a known CV member, he would have admitted it?"

"Oui. He would have had no reason to withhold that information."

"I'd be so much more useful if I could watch the actual interviews and understand what they were saying."

"I will have one more of those for you. After we last spoke, I received word that a former CV member has surrendered in Nova Scotia. She was not on the list in the suicide note. When I receive the interview, I will send it on to you."

"Thanks. I'll let you get back to work."

"Au revoir, Jared."

***

Transcripts from the remaining interviews yielded an assortment of admissions and denials, leaving Jared more frustrated.

"Rita, open John Carter's travel records." Pages appeared on the wall. "Rita, summerize."

"John Carter has traveled to every continent and the moon."

Where do I start? Jared drummed his fingers on the desk. "Show his travel on a map of the Earth."

A globe appeared on the wall, rotating. Green lines indicated flights, red ground travel, and blue excursions on the water. Carter had spent the least time in Asia and Antarctica. Lines criss-crossed all the other continents, most of them red.

He's old-fashioned, like me. He wants to see the country. That means he could have run into a CV member anywhere along these lines.

"Rita eliminate air and water travel." The lines disappeared. "Superimpose homes of known CV members, both living and deceased."

Black dots appeared on the globe, concentrated in France and western Switzerland. *As expected.* One of the punishments for convicted extremists had been restriction to their country of origin.

Carter might have traveled so much because he knew that would stop if he was ever found out.

"Just show the map of Europe." He studied it for some time. *This is useless. He could have crossed paths with dozens of CV members there.* "Show North America." Something caught his eye. "Narrow search to Canada. Did Carter take a CP Rail trip across Canada?"

"Yes, Chief."

Jared gazed at the lines. Only a handful of CV members had been located in Canada, most in Quebec. *There could be others.* Quebec would be a good place for a French fugitive to blend in. Or a native of Quebec could have gotten caught up in the CV when visiting France.

That's not it. What's bothering me about this map? He sat up straighter, squinting. "Rita, when was Carter's trip to Yukon Province?"

"Three years ago."

"Add the Yukon residence of Lloyd Desjarlais." *I'm really grasping at straws.*

The dot appeared on top of one of Carter's ground travel lines.

"Rita, am I crazy to suspect Desjarlais just because Carter traveled through the town where he lived."

"You have shown no sign of insanity, Chief. Lloyd Desjarlais lived in a city of only five thousand residents. John Carter spent thirty-eight hours there. I am checking their receipts. Both men were at the same restaurant, the Caribou Lodge, at the same time."

"Really? That's still not enough to accuse Lloyd of being a mass murderer. Give me everything in his background from the time he was born."

The records appeared. Jared examined the birth certificate from Thunder Bay, Ontario. Four years later, records moved from Thunder Bay to Hamiliton.

"Show me all school pictures through secondary school graduation."

Several dozen appeared on the wall, from class pictures to extra-curricular activities. In some of the later photos, Jared could recognize the man he knew.

"Rita, does facial recognition confirm that all of these are Lloyd Desjarlais?"

"Yes, Chief."

"Was there any gap between graduation from secondary school and enrollment in university?"

"Mr. Desjarlais enrolled in the University of Toronto the same year he graduated from secondary school."

"Show me any pictures from his tenure there."

Fewer pictures appeared, mostly group pictures of the geology and business clubs. Graduation pictures when Desjarlais earned his bachelors and masters degrees.

Jared could see, without computer assistance, that this was the man he knew. "Work history."

"Desjarlais began working for Sequent Mining in Louisiana two months after graduation. Three years later, he transferred to

Quebec. After five years, he was promoted and moved to Yukon. Several promotions followed, keeping him in the same location until he transferred here."

Jared sighed. "A thoroughly documented history with no missing years. Well, I had to check it out. I won't tell him that I suspected he was an extremist and mass-murderer. Call Captain Julian."

After the usual delay, Renee appeared. "Tell me you have found something."

"I wish I could. I'm sure you noticed that Carter traveled everywhere."

"Oui. That is why I assigned you the task. I thought since you have nothing else to do, you could find something that one of us might miss."

Jared chuckled. "What do you mean? I'm a very busy man."

"Did your department arrest *anyone* since we last talked?"

"No." He grinned. "When someone questions Carter again, zero in on Canada."

"What did you discover?"

"Nothing. It's just an educated guess. Or maybe grasping at straws. Looking at his travels in Europe is useless. Too many trips. Too many former CV members. Other than North America, the other continents have too few known CV members. He took a train ride across Canada and three other trips just to Quebec."

"An ideal place for a CV fugitive to hide. I will conduct the interview and send you a video. Thank you, mon ami. We are running out of leads."

Chapter 14

Two days later, Jared received a video of the John Carter interview. He rushed to open it.

Renee told Carter that she had some follow-up questions. Jared watched Carter relax as she made harmless inquiries about known CV members.

"Which CV members did you see in Canada?"

Carter stiffened just enough to notice. "Why do you ask?"

"Why do I *ask?* It is my job to ask. It is your job to answer. Who did you see?"

"Why, no one."

"You are lying."

Carter shifted in his seat. "I tell you, I saw no one. Address any further questions to my barrister."

The interview ended. Renee's face appeared. "Of course, he is lying. I have sent out a bulletin to the RCMP. They will notify all law enforcement agencies where Carter traveled. There are one or more unknown CV members in Canada."

"I guess it feels good to know I was on the right track."

***

The interview of the Nova Scotia CV member was waiting for him when he reached his office the next morning. The woman who appeared on the screen looked too young to have been a CV member.

The interviewer began. "State your name."

"Marie Garçon."

"How old were you when you joined the CV?"

"Fourteen."

"Why did you join?"

"My mother and her boyfriend joined. She did not want me to become involved, but he insisted. He was a fanatic."

"What was your mother's name?"

"Antoinette Garçon."

"How did you escape the crackdown?"

"Maman had taken another girl and I into the woods to pick berries. She saw the soldiers and hid us till they passed. Then we ran away as fast as we could. We heard the shooting and the explosions. I asked about my little brother. My friend asked about her parents and sister. Maman said we could do nothing for them. We had to save ourselves."

"Where did you go?"

"A small town outside of Paris where we had relatives. There we learned that the children were safe. I wanted to go get Pierre, but Maman said that we could not. The relatives we were staying with found the other girl's grandparents. Later I heard that they also took custody of her sister."

"And you?"

"My uncle lived here. We emigrated to Canada."

"Did you ever see your brother again?"

"Last year. After Maman died. She is the reason I surrendered. I think she may have died from that poison."

"Why do you believe that?"

"Two years ago, she started having breathing problems. She saw a number of doctors, specialists. None could determine the cause. She was able to continue her daily routine with supplemental oxygen. She believed the problem was caused by handling explosives without proper protective equipment. Of course, she could not tell the doctors that. After these other murders, I wonder ..."

"When did her condition deteriorate?"

"Perhaps a month before she died. Of course, she told no one at first. She simply increased the oxygen. When she told her doctor, he ran more tests, changed medications, the usual treatment. She entered hospital a week later and died within days."

"In the days leading up to her initial diagnosis, did she mention seeing any former CV members? Had you seen any?"

"I have seen no one from that time, other than on the news after an arrest." Her brow furrowed. "Un fantôme. She said she saw a ghost."

"Did she explain?"

"She said she saw someone who had been reported killed in the crackdown. I tried to get her to tell me more. She said it was safer for me if I did not know." Tears ran down her cheeks. "Why did I not think of this when Maman became ill? Why did the tests not detect the poison?"

"Routine tests would not have detected it. And there was no antidote. Torturing yourself like this is futile."

The interviewer asked a few more questions, but Garçon provided no more useful information. Jared considered the implications.

This makes Antoinette Garçon victim one. Maybe even an experiment to check the lethal dose. That could explain the gap between initial symptoms and her terminal decline. Did the killer come back to finish her off?

"Un fantôme." He said the words aloud. Rita knew he was talking to himself again and did not respond. *Someone who everyone thought was killed in the crackdown. Our suspect pool just got a lot bigger.*

"Incoming message from Captain Julian," Rita said.

"Play."

Renee appeared. "I knew that after seeing the Garçon interview you would want this information. Samples collected during her mother's autopsy contain the poison. The test for it was also conducted on samples from her regular medical appointments. The levels remained constant until three months before her death, when they increased dramatically. I believe the killer returned to finish the job."

"Call Captain Julian."

When Renee appeared live, she smiled. "That did not take long."

"You realize that our suspect pool just exploded?"

"I have studied the raid extensively. After the crackdown, pictures were taken of the bodies. We confirmed with DNA tests."

"What about explosions? Marie Garçon mentioned explosions."

"Yes. Both the CV and our soldiers threw grenades. The bomb factory was destroyed in a massive explosion."

"There must have been some bodies too mutilated to identify."

"Yes. Again, DNA was used."

"That's the list we need to look at."

"I will have my computer search the files for any CV members identified by DNA only. You will get the list as soon as I have it."

   ***

When Jared received the list, he shook his head. *I thought it would be short.* The bomb factory had been housed in an old barn. The massive blast had resulted in three secondary explosions. Twenty-six CV members had been identified by DNA tests only. The vast majority of remains—twenty-one—were not intact enough to call them bodies.

That's twenty-one new suspects. Among them, Henri's wife and father-in-law. *I need to talk to Rachelle again.* He checked the time.

"Rita, prepare video message for Rachelle Le Claire."

"Ready to record."

"Good day, Rachelle. I have a couple more questions for you. Call me at your convenience. Rita, send message."

***

The call came minutes later.

"Bon jour, Chief. Have you made progress finding Papa's killer?"

"We're no closer to the killer's identity. But we've collected a lot more information. It will all lead us there."

"I know now that authorities here *do* care about finding justice for Papa and the other victims. That is reassuring. But I still prefer talking to you. Papa was your friend. It matters more to you."

"You can count on that. Rachelle, I have a very tough question for you."

Rachelle took a deep breath and let it out. "Proceed."

"Over the years, did anything ever lead you to believe that your mother or grandfather survived the attack?"

Rachelle stared. "Why would you ask such a thing?"

"You deserve an answer to that. We've just discovered the first victim of this killer. Shortly before she started showing symptoms, she told her daughter that she had seen a ghost—a CV member who everyone thought was killed during the attack. Your mother and grandfather were among about twenty who were identified only by DNA."

"I understand." She nodded. "I never saw either of them again. However, each Christmas I received an unmarked present. I told my great-aunt that they were from Maman, that she was hiding somewhere. She let me believe that until I turned fifteen. Then she told me they were most likely from Papa, that if Maman were alive she would have found some way to see me."

"Did you believe her?"

"Not at first. I rebelled at the thought. But after considering it for two more years, I accepted it."

"How long did the gifts continue?"

"Through my university graduation. There were secondary school and university graduation gifts as well. And a wedding present when we married."

"Did you ever try to discover the source of these gifts?"

"Yes. But you know how difficult that is without the proper resources."

"Sometimes, even with the resources. Did you ask your father about them?"

Rachelle hesitated and her eyes glistened. "I meant to. I kept forgetting."

"I'll see what I can find out for you. I know this wasn't easy. I'll let you go now."

"Thank you, Chief. Please, call if you need anything else."

"I will. Rita, end call. You heard the conversation. What can you do about tracking down the source of those presents?"

"Searching Henri Le Claire's financial records for purchases delivered to Rachelle Le Claire. If he did not make the purchases, I have little recourse until you have other financial records to search."

"I understand."

"Purchases found. The two graduation gifts and the wedding gift were sent by Henri Le Claire."

"None of the others. Check the financial records of Rachelle's other living relatives—aunts, uncles, grandparents."

The search took Rita a few minutes. "No results found."

Jared leaned back in his seat. *This doesn't prove that Michelle Le Claire survived the attack. Like the aunt said, she would have found a way to see her daughter. A mother would. The gifts might have been sent by another survivor. Someone close to Michelle. Michelle's mother's body was identified, but not her father's. He could have been sending presents to his granddaughter.*

"Rita, prepare a video message for Captain Julian."

Jared recorded the message, telling Renee what he had learned, then called it a day.

Chapter 15

The hunt for the CV serial killer, as the media called him, stalled.

Jared welcomed the distraction of planning for Joel's visit.

An Air Force flight attempting to set a new speed record was enough of a special occasion to invite dignitaries to Armstrong Base. Jared and Karen took the day off. They watched on television as the S-7 spacecraft separated from Shepard Spaceport, used retro-rockets to maneuver clear, then engaged its plasma engine.

The S-7 had set the last three Earth-to-moon speed records. Engineers continued to tweak its design to make it faster. It had already shaved forty minutes off the average trip. If the difference could be increased to an hour, it would begin replacing the current interplanetary ships.

Jared tucked his coffee cup into the dish sterilizer. "I'll take our spacesuits to the shuttle bay, then check in with Lars before we leave."

"This place won't fall apart if you're gone overnight." Karen wrapped her arms around his shoulders. "Lars can handle anything that comes up."

"I know. I know. I'm just killing time till our flight. I'll be back in an hour."

Karen chuckled. "Don't make me wait for you."

***

Jared enjoyed this trip to Armstrong more than most, due to Karen's company and the promise of Joel's visit. After the base commander formally welcomed the dignitaries, Jared and Karen checked into their guest quarters. Then he took her along to his monthly meeting with the head of security.

Periodic announcements over the station's intercom updated everyone on the progress of the S-7's flight.

They returned to their quarters in time to change for the landing.

Karen removed her evening gown and Jared's dress uniform from the press. The latest in wrinkle-removing technology, all lunar guest quarters included one. It looked like a narrow closet. Hang wrinkled garments inside, wait at least ten minutes, and they came out looking freshly pressed.

"Thanks for taking me to your meeting. I got to see parts of the base that aren't on the usual tour."

"You can come along with me to any of the other bases and get the same access. There's not much off-limits to Lunar Enforcement."

"I might just do that. We'd better get ready. Don't want to be late for Joel's big day."

They changed and hurried to the interplanetary landing bay with a permanent platform and seating for welcoming ceremonies.

Jared shook hands with an Asian couple, then introduced them to Karen. "Karen, these are Drs. Sara and Shin Kim. My wife, Karen."

Shin took Karen's hand in both of his. "Dr. Mason-Pearce, it is so nice to finally meet you. I have read several of your papers."

"Thank you. Please call me Karen." She turned to Sara. "You must be so excited to see your daughter."

"Just giddy." Sara shook her hand. "And we're so proud of Wanda. She and your son, Joel, have become close friends."

Karen hesitated. "I guess that's the difference between sons and daughters. He's barely said a thing about the other members of the crew." She chuckled. "Now that you mention it, we have no idea who his friends are."

"Typical man."

An officer directed the parents to seats in the front row. They watched on a monitor as the S-7 began its descent.

Jared checked the time. This flight would set a new record. But by how much?

When the S-7 touched down, the clock stopped. Almost twelve minutes better than the previous mark. Dignitaries and Armstrong residents applauded.

Docking took several minutes. A camera showed the airlock. The S-7's door opened and the flight crew disembarked. Ground crew members began helping them out of their spacesuits.

"There's Wanda," Sara said.

Karen half-stood, then settled. "There's Joel."

Jared wrapped his arm around her shoulders. "Be patient. Just a few more minutes."

The crew finished and the airlock opened. Applause erupted again. The four parents in the audience led a standing ovation. Wanda Kim blushed and shook her head. Joel smiled and touched the cross hanging from his neck.

Jared nodded. When Joel had entered the Air Force Academy, he had told his parents that this would be his greeting to them. An "everything okay" signal when he could not talk.

After the crew took seats behind a podium, the base commander welcomed them and introduced each to the audience. The mission commander gave a brief statement. Then the crew was dismissed to change from their flight suits.

While the crowd disbursed, Jared led Karen and the Kims to greet their children.

Karen wrapped her son in a long hug. "It's been so long."

"I know, Mom, but I need a shower. Don't hug me when you're all dressed up."

"I don't care." She released him.

Jared shook his hand. "I'll hug you later. Great to see you, son."

"This would be stellar even if you weren't here." Joel grinned. "I want to introduce you to Wanda."

"Her mom tells us that you're good friends. News to us."

"Yeah, well ... you know." He turned toward the Kims, who were speaking excited Korean.

Karen grabbed Joel's left hand. "Is that an engagement ring?"

"Well, yeah."

Sara looked up from examining her daughter's hand. "They're engaged!"

Karen bounced. "We just found out too."

Jared stood back watching everyone. The mothers hugged each other. Joel wrapped his arm around Wanda's waist. Shin grinned.

"Dad," Joel said. "How do you feel about this?"

Jared smiled. "It's not bad enough my son chose the Air Force over the Navy. Now my daughter-in-law is an airman too. Welcome to the family."

Wanda hugged him, then Karen. "Joel has told me so much about you. I want to get to know you better, but we really need to go change for the banquet tonight. We'll all be at the same table, so we can talk then."

Joel and Wanda departed. The parents stood for an awkward moment.

Jared broke the silence. "Well, I sure wasn't expecting that."

"Nor was I," Shin said. "But it is welcome news."

Sara wiped tears away. "I suspected that they were more than just friends. You know, mother/daughter talks. I thought they might tell us that. But I wasn't expecting an engagement. Their rings are beautiful."

"We all got a lot more than we bargained for." Jared grinned. "No shortage of things to talk about during the banquet."

***

That evening, Joel, Wanda, and their parents had a table to themselves. Mayors from the settlements took their turns at the podium, welcoming the crew. Then each of the airmen said a few words.

Finally, they settled down to eating and visiting.

Karen asked the question on everyone's mind. "Have you set a date?"

Wanda answered. "Since your vacations overlap the second week in September, we've already booked the Academy chapel. I sent out invitations after we told you. It will be a dress uniform ceremony. We'll *both* be in uniform. No wedding dress for me."

"Oh-h." Sara could not hide her disappointment.

"Mom, does this really surprise you?"

"No. I hoped you would change your mind when the time came."

Joel squeezed Wanda's hand. "Whatever she wants. We've already taken the marriage classes, and the parenting classes. We both plan to continue our careers and hold off having kids for a couple of years."

"And," Wanda said. "We may decide to use a surrogate at that time. Restrictions have been relaxed for pregnant airmen, but there are still a few reasonable limitations. I'm not sure if I'll be ready to accept them. And we don't want to wait till we retire to have kids."

"Good," both mothers said in unison.

Jared chuckled. "If you have kids, I might get out of here in less than ten years."

Joel pointed at him. "Don't count on it, Dad. We both plan to apply to NASA next year. We'd both like to live here. With our experience, we should go to the top of the list."

"*Sure*. Get my hopes up, then crush them."

"Dad, you're the only person I know who wouldn't like to live on the moon."

"Of course. You hang around with a bunch of fly-boys." Jared flashed a smile. "At least forty percent of the people who come here to work fulfill their one-year contract, then they're gone. It's growing on me, but I miss horses. And dogs."

"Your father is correct," Shin said. "We have a similar turnover at North Pole. Many people come here for the easy money. With few expenses, a couple can save enough in one year to buy a house."

Joel and Wanda looked from one father to the other.

Wanda addressed her parents. "Mom and Dad, do you feel that way?"

"Oh, no," Sara said. "Our apartment here is bigger than the one we had in Seoul. We like living in a small town where everyone knows you. There are more parks and opportunities for recreation. We plan to stay here till we retire, then buy a big house in Arizona."

"Jared is the odd man out in this group." Karen patted his hand. "I love it here too. Fortunately, he loves me enough to put up with it."

Jared kissed her. "And the money's great."

***

The next morning, Jared and Karen returned to Tranquility, knowing they would see Joel and Wanda again in seventy-two hours.

Upon his arrival, Jared resumed his duties. Lars gave him a report on the past twenty-four hours—nothing had happened—then Jared called Renee for progress on the CV case. Nothing there either.

Jared sighed. *It's not just that I want to catch Henri's killer.* He had to admit that he missed the action. *I enjoy the hunt.* He shrugged, then smiled. *Maybe I should start writing mysteries. I have the time.*

He made his way to the farm and wandered around, looking at the crops, thinking of Henri. *I will catch your killer, Henri. I won't fail at this.*

He shook his head and pushed the thoughts out of his mind. *Enough of that. I need to concentrate on Joel's visit.*

***

The Air Force shuttle arrived to much fanfare. Because the base air locks were not equipped for crowds, most people watched the landing on large screens at the soccer field.

Jared and Karen were among a handful who greeted the crew at the airlock, then escorted them to the field. Each of the crew members addressed the gathering before Jared and Karen had Joel and Wanda to themselves for a couple hours.

Later, Jared took them to the school to answer questions from students. Joel and Wanda were assigned the first and second-graders. He watched them interact with the youngsters. *They'll be good parents. They have a lot of patience.*

That evening, while the rest of the crew dined with base management, Joel and Wanda were allowed a private dinner with Jared and Karen at *Earth View.*

Jared pulled out Karen's chair for her. "I guess you've told everyone that you're engaged."

Joel took his seat. "They all got invitations. Wanda would smack me if I did that for her."

"I realize that you have to follow military protocol, but, Wanda, let him be a gentleman if it's appropriate. There's too little of that anymore."

"Yes, sir." Wanda dropped her eyes. "When someone does something like that, I feel like they're telling me that I can't do it myself."

"I see. Karen, is that how you feel?"

She laughed. "Wanda, if Joel acts like a gentlemen, think of it this way. He knows you're totally capable of doing it yourself. He just thinks you're special and shouldn't have to. That's how we raised him."

"Oh-h. My dad isn't like that. But, then, Mom would probably smack him too."

"That's the way most people are these days."

***

The next morning, Wanda and Karen spent time talking about wedding plans while Jared took Joel on patrol with him.

"Dad, I haven't really had time to talk to you about your friend—Henri. I know you were close."

"Yes, we were. He knew I was a farm boy from the minute I met him. The farm is still my favorite place."

"I only met him once, but I know you meant a lot to him."

"You met him? When?"

"After you talked about him. You mentioned his lunar farming courses. I thought it would be entertaining. The first one was so interesting, I took another. The course said I could e-mail him with questions. After I told him who I was, he asked to video chat. We must have talked for a half-hour. He was a nice man."

"Yes, he was. It's frustrating that we can't catch his killer."

"Any progress at all?"

The door slid open before them and Jared inhaled the smells of the farm. "Toward catching the killer, no. But a lab did develop a treatment for the poison."

"An antidote?"

"Too soon to tell." Chickens moved off the path in front of them. "People who ingested low doses of the poison have no traces of it in their system after taking the treatment. More severe cases are improving. Doctors say it will take another month to determine if it's a cure or just a treatment."

"I haven't heard of any new cases."

"I'm in the loop and I'm not aware of any either."

"Does it bother you being here, when all the action is happening on Earth?"

"Yes."

"Do you resent being here?"

Jared stopped and stared at his son. "No. Your mom sacrificed a lot for me. She had to turn down a couple of good jobs because I was gone so much. She turned this job down *three times*. I'm right where I belong. But thanks for reminding me."

Chapter 16

After the Air Force shuttle left, Jared needed a distraction even more. He threw himself into his job. He welcomed the chance to review a new group of workers still in quarantine.

Taurus had the majority again—a dozen. Four would stay at Apennine, North Pole had four, Armstrong Base three, and eight would come to Tranquility.

Jared checked the local list. Married geologists from the United Kingdom with three school-age children caught his eye. *Outstanding. Everybody likes to see more kids in school.* A woman from Quebec would manage the night club. Then he recognized a name. Allison Desjarlais. *It must have gotten hot enough in New Orleans for Lloyd's wife to get out of there.* The final man was an engineer from India.

Reviewing thirty-one personnel files took most of the reminder of the morning. Jared checked the time. *Just enough to make my weekly call to Renee before I meet Karen for lunch.* "Rita, call Captain Julian."

Renee smiled when she saw him. "Nothing worth reporting, mon ami."

"You would have called me if there was." Jared shrugged. "But I feel like I should contact you at least once a week."

"I am happy that you did. I said there is nothing worth reporting, but Canadian authorities did find an elderly former CV member. When Carter traveled through there, the man was hospitalized due to severe injuries. He has been in a retirement home since."

"So it's not likely that he was the person Carter saw but wouldn't talk about."

"Unlikely. That is not the only reason I am happy that you called. I have discussed the matter with my superiors and they told me to ask you. Would you be interested in a consulting position with Interpol?"

Jared leaned forward. "Tell me more."

"You could work from there. You said that you are also fluent in Spanish and Italian?"

"You could say that." He smiled. "I understand fluently. I often speak slowly because I'm sometimes still thinking in English."

"That is satisfactory for this position. It would involve familiarizing yourself with a case, then watching interviews. You have picked up on things we missed. You could again. We may not call on you every week. You would simply be another set of eyes when we need assistance. You would be well-paid."

Jared chuckled. "I'm already making more money than I'll ever use. If I accept this offer, it will be because I'm bored. I'm very interested. But I have to talk to Karen and my bosses. Have your bosses send me a contract to review."

Renee pushed a button. "Done. They are quite enthusiastic about this idea. They spoke to others who worked with you during your tenure with the Naval Criminal Investigative Service. They wanted more opinions than mine."

"I would expect that. You may not hear from me for a couple of days. In the meantime, you can pass along my interest."

"Very good, mon ami. Until then." Renee disconnected.

"Rita, review the contract Renee sent. We'll discuss it after lunch."

"Yes, Chief."

Jared smiled. Computers had reduced the need for lawyers. Most people considered that a good thing. He bounded from his chair, left the office and descended the stairs four at a time. On the ground floor he slowed to a walk en route to the corporate cafeteria.

When he reached it, he saw Lloyd before he found Karen.

The boss smiled. "Hello, Chief. Having lunch with Karen today?"

"Yeah. I've been in the office all morning. I see your wife has arrived."

The smile widened. "Finally. I can't wait for you to meet her. Will we be having lunch again?"

"All my new residents get the same treatment. What will she do to keep herself busy here?"

"Decorating our apartment first. She shipped three cases of things from Earth. I have reserved a garden plot for her. She loves gardening. She will be teaching some art classes and is interested in sculpting with lunar materials."

"She'll be a welcome addition to our community."

"I hope she likes it here."

"If she doesn't, have her talk to me. I've found ways to appreciate it. I know you're excited, but as one of my bosses, I need to bounce something off you."

Lloyd took a deep breath and assumed a more businesslike expression. "Go on."

"Interpol has offered me a side job as a consultant. I can work from here. It probably wouldn't be every week. I won't do it without the board's approval."

Lloyd nodded. "The board meets by video conference tomorrow. I'll put it on the agenda. I think they all know how over-qualified you are for this job. I need Karen, therefore I want to keep you happy. I *will* get their approval."

"Thanks, Lloyd. You don't have to worry about me leaving until Karen's ready. But I think I won't feel so restless if I have something more challenging to occupy my mind. I have to discuss this with her yet."

"I understand. There's Karen now. I'll leave you to your lunch."

Lloyd departed and Jared kissed Karen. "Lloyd's really excited about seeing his wife."

Karen chuckled. "He's been showing pictures of her and their two boys to everyone."

"I thought she might be too uppity for this rock, but he says she likes gardening so she can't be all bad."

"Let's get our lunch. I'm starving. Have you looked up her sculptures?"

"No."

"She does pretty good sketches and charcoal drawings, but her sculptures are gorgeous."

Jared ordered his meal. "Maybe the board will commission her to do artwork for the settlements. That will give her something to do."

"That's a great idea. We could use more sculptures." They took seats at a quiet table. "Lloyd has really loosened up in the past few weeks."

"He went from standoffish to friendly. I wouldn't call him a friend yet, but we're getting there." Jared moved salad around the plate with his fork.

"You look like you're about to burst. What's going on?"

Jared grinned. "Interpol offered me a consulting job. I can work from here. I wouldn't have even considered it otherwise."

"Oh-h, that's perfect. What do you think the board will say?"

"I was talking to Lloyd about that before you got here. He said he'll convince the others that it's in everyone's best interest to keep me happy."

"Absolutely. Including mine."

"So I guess you're okay with this."

Karen squeezed his hand. "I know you're bored out of your mind half the time. This sounds horrible, but you've been more like your old self since Henri's murder. It's like you have a purpose again. A consulting job is so much better than more murders here."

"Much." A sad smile flashed, then disappeared. "I've caught myself enjoying the investigation, then felt guilty."

"I understand. It's what you're best at."

***

Jared returned to his office feeling better than he had in a long time. "Rita, how did the contract look to you?"

"It is a modified Interpol inspector's contract."

"What?"

"It is an Interpol inspector's contract, modified to an 'on-call only' status. It would make you Interpol's inspector on the moon."

Jared's brow furrowed. "Renee said that it was a consultant's contract."

"It does mention consulting on non-lunar cases from your base of operations here."

"Is there anything that would interfere with my LEO duties?"

"It specifically prohibits that. Any lunar cases which on Earth would fall under the jurisdiction of Interpol, would become joint investigations. This can only benefit Lunar Enforcement."

"Do you see any downside to this contract?"

"There is a three hundred, sixty-five day a year clause. You can request time off, but you could still be interrupted while on vacation. Another clause requires you to meet with your superiors for no more than four hours during your annual leave on Earth."

"I can work with both of those requirements. I suppose the board will want to see the contract before they let me sign it. No point in worrying about it until I hear what they have to say."

***

The Lunar Governing Board requested a copy of the contract before their meeting. They also asked that Jared be ready to join them by video. He stayed busy in his office until Rita summoned him.

"The Lunar Governing Board requests that you join their video conference."

"Put me in."

The five board members appeared on Jared's wall. Robert Yamashita, the board president, spoke for the others. "Thank you for joining us, Chief."

"Thanks for considering this."

"I have a tough question for you. Are you threatening to quit if we don't agree to this?"

Jared knew from the expressions of the other board members that this was Yamashita's concern alone.

"That would be pretty stupid of me. I have a half-dozen officers who could step into my job seamlessly. But being chief of Lunar Enforcement involves mostly organization and public relations. I will be much happier in my job if I get to use my investigative skills more often."

Lloyd cleared his throat. "As I said."

Yamashita waved an impatient hand. "Yes. However, the question needed to be asked. All members in favor of allowing the chief to take on a second job as Interpol inspector, say aye." The vote was unanimous. "Motion passed. Congratulations on your new job, Chief."

"Thank you."

The other members were offering their congratulations when the connection ended.

Jared shook his head. "Yamashita, you old grouch."

***

When Jared called Renee to tell her that he had accepted the lunar inspector's position, it surprised her.

"I was told that it was a consultant's contract. I had no idea."

"That's okay. But it was quite a shock when Rita told me."

"Of course. When you consider the matter, it makes perfect sense. Interpol can now say we have an inspector on the moon if an investigation leads there. And it lends credibility to your organization."

"Some people still think we're a bunch of security guards."

"No one who has ever been there, I assume."

"No. They usually don't make that mistake even once."

"Expect much fanfare with this announcement. Perhaps even a televiscd swearing-in ceremony."

Jared scowled. "I'd like to skip that part."

"I am certain that it is in the contract."

"Rita, is there anything in that contract about participating in publicity events?"

"Yes, Chief. I did not mention it because the clause is identical to your Lunar Enforcement contract."

Renee could not stop laughing.

Jared pointed at her. "I'll remember this."

"Of course." She wiped her eyes. "Until next time, mon ami ... Inspector."

    ***

Jared was allowed some input into his swearing-in ceremony. He chose the farm, with fruit trees for a background. Though the event would be broadcast lunar-wide, he limited attendees to his Tranquility officers, Karen, and Lloyd.

The Interpol commander conducted the ceremony from headquarters on Earth.

It all lasted only fifteen minutes, but that was more than enough for Jared. He kissed Karen as the group disbursed. "Now I have to sit for an interview with Regina before I can get back to work."

Karen patted him on top of the head, smiling. "If you're trying to make me feel sorry for you, it's not working."

Jared just laughed.

Chapter 17

Other than a few people calling him "Inspector" in jest, nothing changed for Jared. The week featured his lunches with new arrivals.

He made a point of looking up Allison Desjarlais' artwork before meeting with her and Lloyd.

Allison not only shook the hand Jared offered, she kissed his cheek.

Jared smiled. "You're a lot friendlier than your husband was the first time I met him."

She laughed—a big laugh that turned heads. "Oh, he thought it was a complete waste of time. However, you won him over. You are one of several people he was eager to have me meet."

They chose a table and Jared noted that Lloyd pulled out her chair. "I looked up your artwork. I especially like the sculpture of the eagle fishing."

"Oh, that is Lloyd's favorite also. I brought a casting of it for our apartment."

"How long do you plan to be with us?"

"I do love our place in New Orleans. My gardens especially." She sipped her beverage. "I think I shall return in October. But I will come back here before Mardi Gras next spring. I avoid the French Quarter if I *am* there."

Jared chuckled. "I understand. Can you do anything artistically here that you couldn't do on Earth?"

"I intend to attempt to cast the regolith here. It has been terra-formed into so many smooth shapes. I want to see if it can be pressed into irregular shapes."

"A boost for the economy. Another lunar export. Tourists and people on Earth would love it."

"That would be magnifique. I had no doubt that I could contribute to the culture here. However, I did not feel that was enough. Do you understand?"

Jared nodded. "That's actually pretty common here. Most couples who come both have jobs waiting for them. When one of them doesn't, it takes that person awhile to find their niche and feel like they are contributing. The job they held on Earth may not exist here. Or it may be filled. Doreen, at the store, is a good example. She might seem like just a clerk, but she's actually a certified public accountant."

"That is exactly my situation. Wherever we have lived, I have opened an art gallery. There is no extra space for it here, and a limited supply of patrons."

Jared chewed for a moment, then gestured with his fork. "Talk to Lunar Adventures. It would be the logical place for a gallery. They have a steady supply of buyers."

"Oh, that is a wonderful idea. I will work on a business plan. And it would add a job or two there because I would be here most of the time. I could have shows on occasion. Perhaps that would encourage more art-loving tourists to come here. Yes, that is the perfect idea."

Lloyd smiled. "Thank you, Chief. This will keep her occupied for at least a month."

***

"Incoming call from Captain Julian," Rita said.

Jared's heart rate accelerated. *Our weekly call isn't for three days.* "Put her through. Hello, Renee. Has there been a development?"

"Another CV member has been uncovered in Quebec. The person speaks fluent English, so I have arranged for the interrogation to be conducted in English."

"I appreciate that."

"I believe we have a better chance of solving this case if you witness these interviews."

"I appreciate that too. How did you find this one?"

"By scouring the records of another recently-exposed member. A pattern appeared. The investigator expected to find an extra-marital affair, but proceeded with an open mind."

"That's really important in this case."

"Oui. You need not concern yourself that nothing is being done here. These investigations into background are ongoing."

"I assumed they were. Have the travel records of all CV members been scoured like I did with Carter's?"

"Yes. Each investigator was told to look for travel patterns. I believe that is how the latest member was exposed."

"What about collectively?"

"Ah-h. I see. Very good, mon ami. This will be your assignment. I will send you the travel records of all CV members. Find a pattern."

"Everything from the time they returned to society after the crackdown. Something else occurred to me a couple days ago when I was looking at the case files again. Because of this serial killer, we've uncovered several dozen former CV members."

"Correct. I believe the number stands at thirty-nine."

"Nobody was really searching for them anymore."

"True." Renee nodded. "It was no longer an active case. I believe I see where you are going with this."

"If I was an exposed CV member, I'd be mad as hell at this killer. I was living my new life, probably didn't worry much anymore about being exposed, then he comes along and destroys all that."

"You believe we should conduct follow-up interviews and remind them of that."

"At worst, it can do no harm. At best, we could get more names."

"I will make this happen. Collecting the travel records of all the members may take an hour. You will have them as soon as I do."

"Thanks, Renee."

***

"Rita, display all travel patterns on a globe."

Europe became a mass of green and red. Similar collections appeared in Cairo, Morocco, Quebec, New York, Florida, Phoenix, Los Angeles, Tahiti, and Melbourne. Green, red, and blue lines crossed the rest of the globe.

"Where do I start?"

"Where the lines intersect," Rita replied.

Jared smiled. "Eliminate destinations where less than five CV members traveled. Eliminate those routes."

Most of the globe became less cluttered.

What criteria should I use next? "Show only the travel of Antoinette Garçon." Jared stared at the results. "That's it?"

"The subject flew from Paris to Halifax, then traveled by rail to Belmont, Nova Scotia. She traveled to Halifax several times, then to Montreal once. It was her only trip outside the province."

"Show me the dates of her trips along with the date she first experienced symptoms of the poison." Only one trip to Halifax occurred after she became ill. "How many known CV members traveled through Belmont, Nova Scotia?"

"Twenty-three. It is a popular tourist destination."

Jared's brow furrowed. "How many are now deceased?"

"Fourteen."

"Show me the travel patterns of deceased CV members. Eliminate the places visited by less than five."

Europe still showed a mass of red and green, though not as thick. Only three other places in the world looked like Christmas lights—Morocco, New York, and Montreal.

And Antoinette Garçon didn't travel to Morocco or New York. "How many deceased CV members traveled to Montreal?"

"Seventeen."

"Add any trips made by those who were poisoned, but survived."

"Four of those traveled to Montreal."

"Show the years when those trips occurred ... Huh?"

Most of the deceased CV members had traveled to Montreal more than a decade before. Three had made additional trips later. Another had only traveled there once, three years ago. But his trip coincided with Antoinette's.

"Call Captain Julian."

After the usual delay, Renee's smiling face appeared. "You have found something."

"Montreal." Jared paused for effect. "Seventeen of the twenty-one dead CV members traveled there. Plus four more who were poisoned, but survived."

Renee gaped. "I could kiss you, mon ami."

"It's too soon to celebrate. Other than two, Antoinette Garçon and Dubois, who were there on the same day, most of the trips were more than a decade ago. Three people also made later trips."

"What are you suggesting?"

"Montreal is a popular destination for former CV members, both living and dead. Dozens have visited there who haven't been poisoned. Why this group? Why not the others? I don't think the person responsible for their deaths lives in Montreal anymore."

Renee sagged in her seat. "What about Garçon and Dubois?"

"I sometimes visit places where I used to live. The killer might have done the same. Those two were in the wrong place at the wrong time."

"So we are no closer to the killer."

"Maybe not. But this will all help us connect the murders to a suspect when we have one."

"Oui. Yes, it will. Thank you for all your work."

Jared disconnected and checked the time. "Better not be late for my lunch with Caroline Delhomme."

***

"John Carter is dead." Renee said.

Jared had hoped for good news when Renee called again the next day. "What happened?"

"Murder. An old-fashioned knife. He was stabbed twelve times, only an hour after he was released on bail."

"Images of the killer?"

"Poor ones. Heavily disguised. He pulled Carter into a blind spot, then disposed of his clothing in another before disappearing into a crowd. Computers are working to enhance the images. We are testing the clothing for DNA."

Jared slammed his fist on the desk. "I *knew* he saw someone. He wouldn't tell us and it got him killed. He was in Montreal during the same time frame as the others. We could have had the killer in custody."

"Oui. I believe it is significant that the killer used a knife rather than poison."

"No time. Carter had to be eliminated fast. If you catch the guy with the knife, he will probably turn out to be a hit man."

"Quite possible. Let us hope that he is captured alive. And soon."

"Even if he's not captured alive, we should be able to track his payment back to its source."

"God willing."

"Yes. I need to remind myself of that. Keep me posted."

"You will know more the moment I do."

Jared disconnected, then slammed his fist on the desk again.

"Chief, you are angry," Rita said. "Can I do anything to help you feel better?"

Despite his mood, Jared had to smile. *Computers have come a long way.* "Thank you, Rita. But you're doing all you can. I think the only thing that will help me feel better is catching the CV killer."

"Based on the progress we have made, you could be angry for some time. That is not good for you."

"You're right. Send Karen a message. 'Lunch? At home?' End message." *Karen knows what that means.* "I'll go on patrol until then. Exercise will be good for me."

Chapter 18

Jared flopped down on the bed, sweating and breathing hard. "Thanks. I needed that."

Karen snuggled into his arms. "So, what brought this on?"

"One of the CV members knew the killer's identity ... We knew he knew it but couldn't get him to tell us ... He was murdered."

"That's a familiar reason."

Jared glanced at her. "Huh?"

"For 'lunch at home.' Witness who won't say what he knows, knowing the criminal but not being able to prove it, interference in your investigation. All common reasons for 'lunch at home.'"

Jared chuckled. "Can't I just love my wife so much that I want a nooner?"

"That's not 'lunch at home.' That's 'I love you. How about we have lunch at home today?' Big difference."

"I see that now. Sorry for using you to work off my frustration."

"Oh, I'm not complaining. It spices things up a little. I like being in bed with a wild man once in awhile."

"Is that right? At least I know you're not getting bored."

"I just have one question."

"What's that?"

"How did you relieve your frustration when you were stationed on an aircraft carrier?"

He laughed. "I lifted weights. And not just for work-related frustration. I lifted weights a lot. Thanks for helping. I should be able to concentrate on my work this afternoon. We'd better have that lunch so you're not late for work."

***

"We are closing in on the man who killed John Carter," Renee said without introduction the next day.

Jared's heart accelerated "CV?"

"No. Michael Lange, a lifelong Londoner. Convictions on lesser charges. A person of interest in three other stabbing deaths. As you said, likely a murderer for hire. The computer matched his mug shot to the surveillance images. Scotland Yard has located him and will try to make an arrest."

"I wish I was there."

"As do I, mon ami. This case spans two continents and the moon. We cannot take part in every operation."

"Thanks for reminding me of that. Speaking of reminders, what about the interview of the CV member captured in Quebec?"

"I may have that later today. He refused to speak without *his* attorney present and his attorney was on holiday. She became available this morning ... Incoming call from Scotland Yard. You may listen in ... Go ahead, Inspector."

"The subject chose to shoot it out. He is deceased. We are commencing a search of his flat."

Jared sagged in his chair. *Don't be so discouraged. They should still be able to track his payment for the job.*

Renee's voice interrupted his thoughts. "Thank you, Inspector. Keep me apprized. End call. Ah, well, we did not get the result we hoped for. However, this is the first connection we have to our CV killer."

"That's a big step. It's the first real progress we've made in quite a while."

"Oui. Ah, already a message from Inspector Cook. Bundles of currency. New bills. In a new backpack. The hit man may have taken his payment the old-fashioned way."

"That makes it harder for us." Jared sighed. "But maybe not, with all the cameras everywhere. If he picked up the money, someone had to drop it off. We might get lucky."

"I am certain that Scotland Yard has given images of the backpack to their computer. They will find when Lange first appears with it."

"We'll just have to wait for more information. Thanks, Renee."

***

That afternoon, Jared received the video from Quebec. The former CV member had gray hair and a beard on his long face. The attorney was his daughter. She was a beauty, not looking much like her father.

She reminds me of someone. I'm not sure who.

She spoke for him. "My client and I have reviewed your evidence. He concedes that long ago he belonged to the *Cause Vertueuse*. He left France before the crackdown. His travel records will confirm that."

"How long before?" the female interrogator asked.

"Weeks. He does not remember the exact date."

"Were you aware of his membership?"

The daughter almost succeeded in suppressing a smile. "Of course not. I would have been obligated to report it."

"Of course. As I am certain you are aware, we are searching for the killer of twenty-one former CV members. This killer also belonged to the CV. We need names before others die."

"Sergeant." The daughter shook her head. "How many CV members did the government kill? A hundred? How do we know this is not a ploy to lure out the others?"

"Mademoiselle Fontaine, no one has actively sought former CV members in over a decade. It was determined that if they had become contributing members of society, there was no reason to pursue them. Your father's involvement may have never come to light. This killer changed all that."

"My client also concedes that point."

Jared saw the interrogator's head turn toward the elder Fontaine. "Help us find the killer."

For the first time, he spoke. "I have seen the names and faces in the news—those killed and those arrested. I recognized a number of each. Over the decades I have seen a handful of former members, briefly." He glanced toward his daughter, on his left. "No one more than once. No one who I remembered by name." He glanced at her again. "I am terribly sorry. I would help you if I could."

The interrogator changed her approach, with no better results. The interview ended.

"He's lying. Rita, scour Philippe Fontaine's financial records. Show me his travel records."

"Yes, Chief."

Travel records dating back to 2049 appeared. The daughter had been correct. Fontaine immigrated to Quebec a month before the crackdown. He settled in La Prairie, a suburb of Montreal, and stayed close to home the first three years.

For the next two years, he traveled in Canada and the United States. Then he spread out across the globe, though he never returned to Europe. *Pretty typical travel pattern. He probably was in Montreal weekly, if not daily. He could have easily crossed paths with CV members, like he admitted.*

But he lied about saying that he never saw anyone more than once. And about wanting to help us.

"Rita, show me his personal history."

"Yes, Chief."

Fontaine's background before the CV was typical. He joined during college. Jared studied the dates. *He would have been a member at the same time as Henri. He probably knew Michelle and Rachelle. What the heck. It's worth a shot.*

"Rita, compare his purchases to the gifts received by Rachelle Le Claire."

It only took a moment. "A complete match, Chief. All the remaining anonymous gifts were purchased by Philippe Fontaine."

"Yes! Stellar!"

"Do you wish to call Captain Julian?"

"Let's see what else we can find first."

Jared stared at Fontaine's background without seeing it. *Why did he send gifts to Rachelle? He could have been Michelle's boyfriend after Henri left. I'll have to check with Rachelle.*

He shook his head and focused on the records. Fontaine earned a BS degree in chemistry and a masters in inorganic chemistry, then went to work for a pharmaceutical company.

Jared caught his breath. "Show travel records again." He glanced through more recent records. "Just show travel to Nova Scotia." He slammed his fist on the desk. "Call Captain Julian."

"Yes, Chief."

He drummed his fingers until Renee appeared. "Fontaine is our killer."

"He has the credentials for it." Renee nodded. "But so have two others."

"But they weren't in Belmont, Nova Scotia just before Antoinette Garçon started showing symptoms and about two months before her death."

"Sacre Bleu! That provides us with means and opportunity. However, what is his motive?"

"Sometimes, with serial killers, we never understand their motive. But he's the one who sent gifts to Rachelle Le Claire. Maybe he was in love with her mother."

"He is the source of all the gifts?"

"All of the ones not sent by Henri. Even if he wasn't in love with Michelle, they must have been close for him to send gifts to Rachelle."

"This is enough to detain him. The RCMP released him with monitoring after the interview. I will have them take him into custody again."

"I'll show Rachelle a picture of Fontaine about the time of the crackdown. See what she can remember about him."

"Very good. I will speak to you soon."

"Rita, end call. Send a message to Rachelle Le Claire. The same one I used last time."

Rachelle called him an hour later. "I am sorry for the delay, Chief."

"No problem. I want to show you a picture of a man who probably knew your mother. It should be on your screen now."

"Oui. That is Philippe. He was Maman's boyfriend for as long as I remember. He was like a father to me. I remember, I cried when he had to leave. I did not want to let go of him."

"Do you remember why he left?"

"Maman said that he had to go on a mission. After the massacre, I hoped that he would come find me."

"I can tell you that he was the source of most of the anonymous gifts. Henri sent the graduation and wedding presents. Philippe Fontaine sent the rest."

"He cared about me. Thank you, Chief. Does he still live?"

"Yes." Jared took a deep breath. "However, he may be connected to your father's death."

"No-o. Why?"

"We don't know. Or why he would kill twenty-one former CV members. But evidence is pointing us in that direction. If we figure it out, I'll tell you."

"Thank you, Chief. And I thank you for solving the mystery of the gifts."

Chapter 19

"Fontaine was Michelle Le Clair's boyfriend," Jared said to Renee.

Renee sighed. "And he is dead. Suicide."

"No-o." Jared could say nothing else for a moment. "Tell me more."

"He took a massive dose of his own poison. When the RCMP arrived to take him into custody, he was gasping for air. They called paramedics, but he passed before they could reach him. He left a hand-written suicide note."

"What did he say?"

"Quoting, 'I created the poison used on my former comrades. Since the massacre, I suppose I have experienced what is called survivor's guilt. I resented those who survived when so many others perished. I wanted to kill them all, but that is not to be. I can eliminate only one more. Myself.' He signed it. The RCMP has found numerous bottles containing a clear liquid. They are searching his computer."

Jared shifted in his chair. "Does anything bother you about that note?"

"I have had little time to consider it. What did you hear that I missed?"

"I'm not sure. Something just doesn't sound right. I'll have to study it more. This isn't the end of it. Have you looked at Fontaine's travel records?"

"No. I have been too busy with Carter's murder."

"Fontaine never returned to Europe."

"I see. Meaning he has at least one accomplice. Perhaps the same person who hired Carter's killer."

"Any progress there?"

"Perhaps. The computer found no footage of Lange carrying the backpack. However, hours after Carter's murder, a package was delivered to his flat. The computer found the delivery company which is searching its records."

"Is the RCMP questioning Fontaine's daughter? Maybe she'll be willing to admit more now that she doesn't have to protect her father."

"It will be done. They say she is distraught. You will have the interview when I do."

"Is Fontaine's wife still living?"

"Yes. I checked. She is not old enough to have been a CV member."

"You read my mind. Send me a copy of the suicide note in Fontaine's handwriting. I'll see if I can figure out what's bothering me about it."

"Computer, send a photo of the Fontaine suicide note to Inspector Pearce."

"Photo sent," a female voice responded.

"Jared, I hope you find something. Until next time." She disconnected.

"Rita, when the suicide note arrives, display it."

"Yes, Chief."

It appeared a minute later. Jared reread it. *"Survivor's guilt."* *I've never heard of that as motivation for a serial killer. The definition of a serial killer excludes guilt.* "Rita, search historical records. Has a serial killer ever expressed guilt?"

The answer did not take long. "No. Regret is sometimes expressed for getting caught or killing someone in error."

"That's what I thought. Is Fontaine's claim of survivor's guilt a plausible motive for killing twenty-one people?"

"No, Chief. I would call that a lie."

"Why would Fontaine confess to the murders, but lie about his motive?"

"Are you thinking out loud, Chief?"

Jared smiled. "Sort of. I have an idea. I want your analysis."

"The most probable answer is that he is protecting someone else."

"That's what I think. The person with the real motive for wanting these people dead ... The ghost." *Michelle Le Claire.*

Jared shook his head. *Where did that come from? Fontaine was her boyfriend after Henri left. For as long as Rachelle could remember. Fontaine left before the crackdown, so he can't be the ghost Antoinette saw. Michelle told her daughter that Fontaine was leaving on a mission. To find a place for her to hide?*

"Rita, prepare a video message for Captain Julian."

"Ready, Chief."

"Renee, I figured out what's wrong with the suicide note. I've never heard of a serial killer who felt any kind of guilt. I believe Fontaine created the poison. But I believe the person with the motive is the 'ghost' who Antoinette Garçon saw. And I'm starting to wonder if that ghost is Michelle Le Claire. Rita, send message."

***

Jared stood and stretched. "Rita, I'm calling it a day."

"Incoming call from Captain Julian."

"Go ahead."Jared returned to his desk. "I expected to hear from you sooner."

Renee smiled. "*Michelle Le Claire.* I apologize. I laughed when I heard you say the name. Then I considered the source and looked closer at your reasoning. My supervisors don't know you. They will have doubts. However, I trust your judgement."

"I have my own doubts. How much of her remains where found?"

"Computer, access *Cause Vertueuse* crackdown data. What remains were found for extremist Michelle Le Claire?"

"The small finger of her left hand, tissue fragments, and blood."

Renee looked at Jared with raised eyebrows. "She could have easily survived. To my knowledge, that was never considered."

"Did everybody want them to be gone so bad that they stopped looking? Do you know anyone who was involved in the raid?"

"I have a retired friend who took part. I will talk to her. If Michelle Le Claire is the ghost, it would explain why Henri Le Claire was killed, even though he left the CV years before the crackdown. She may have feared that Monsieur Le Claire would recognize her, even with cosmetic surgery. The others, like Antoinette Garçon, may have known that she survived."

"She must be planning some kind of move that would put her in the public eye. Political office? Of course, she may have been planning to kill them for years and it just took Fontaine this long to develop the poison."

"Perhaps. She was a cold-blooded murderer. She was caught on camera a number of times killing law enforcement officers, at least two execution style. I will have the RCMP take a closer look at all women of the proper age in sensitive positions."

"They can eliminate jobs that wouldn't put her in the public spotlight."

"True. Oh, and the package to Lange was brought to the delivery company by a courier company, which is checking their records."

Jared shook his head. "We weren't expecting it to be easy."

***

The next morning, Jared had a message to call Renee at 0900 Zulu. After breakfast he hurried to his office and placed the call.

"Good morning, Jared. I have here with me Captain Brigit Siene, retired. Computer, show Captain Siene."

The screen split and Jared saw the captain, long, gray hair in a braid hanging over her shoulder, short sleeves revealing muscular arms.

"Good morning, Captain."

"Good morning, Inspector. Congratulations on your appointment."

"Thank you."

"Brigit," Renee said. "Tell him what you told me."

"When we realized the minimal remains found, we considered that Michelle Le Claire may have survived. We chose to announce her death to lure her out. She was a zealot. None of us believed that she could simply assimilate into society. She would gather her followers and continue their cause."

Jared nodded. "And try to see her daughter."

"We kept the girl under surveillance for years. But as the remaining zealots staged attacks and were eliminated, we began to consider that Le Claire had died in the raid. People retired. Those who remained stopped looking. If she had not decided to go on a killing spree, she could have remained undetected for life."

"We don't know it's her. That's just my theory."

Siene waved a hand of dismissal. "How many small town police chiefs do you suppose Interpol hires as inspectors?"

"I'm guessing that I could be the first." Jared smiled.

"Indeed." Siene slapped her forehead with the heel of her hand. "I wondered what the organization had come to. Then I researched. And spoke to Renee. You have a valid theory. Le Claire would have no remorse for killing twenty people. She had no qualms about killing innocent bystanders to eliminate her target."

"But that still assumes that she survived."

"A number of us never stopped believing that. When years passed and she did not appear, we grudgingly admitted that we could be wrong. We were not. I feel vindicated. I am certain some of my colleagues will also. Merci."

"Thanks for supporting my theory. Where do we go from here?"

"Canada. I will speak to another retired officer. We will volunteer to go to Canada and work with authorities there. I will pay for my own travel if need be."

Renee shook her head. "I am certain that your assistance will be approved. Jared, we will proceed with plans here. I received the interview of Victoria Fontaine this morning. I have yet to look at it. I will send it to you momentarily."

"Thanks."

Renee and Brigit disappeared. Rita spoke. "Incoming video file from Captain Julian."

"Play it."

Victoria Fontaine appeared on the wall, this time in a private residence. *She doesn't look so beautiful today.* A woman sat beside her, holding her hand. Both had red, puffy eyes.

The female interviewer spoke. "Madam Fontaine, you really need not be here. You have answered my questions."

"My daughter needs me. I will not interfere."

Jared hesitated. "Rita, freeze video." He studied mother and daughter. *Victoria Fontaine doesn't look like her mother either.* "Rita, use facial recognition to compare Victoria Fontaine to her parents. Tell me what percentage of traits she has in common with each."

The process took several minutes. "Victoria Fontaine has twenty-two percent of her father's traits, but only three percent of her mother's."

"Analysis?"

"Philippe Fontaine is Victoria Fontaine's biological father. Jasmine Fontaine is not her biological mother."

He chewed his lower lip. *She still reminds me of someone. Rachelle.* "Compare Victoria Fontaine to Michelle Le Claire."

Rita took only a minute. "Forty-three percent traits in common. Michelle Le Claire is Victoria Fontaine's biological mother."

"Send message to Captain Julian. Michelle Le Claire is Victoria Fontaine's biological mother."

"Message sent."

"Continue video."

"Mademoiselle Fontaine, you no longer need to protect your father. We know he was not working alone. Most of the victims were murdered in Europe and he left there before you were born. Did he tell you anything else that would help us capture his accomplices?"

"No. A number of years ago I became interested in genealogy. I found years where there was no record of him. I asked him about it. He became angry, then relented. He asked me to stop my search. He said that it was best if I did not know. The information could jeopardize my dream of becoming an attorney. I did as he asked."

"After he was arrested, did he—"

"Incoming call from Captain Julian," Rita said.

"Freeze video. Put her through."

Both Renee and Brigit appeared, grinning, speaking excited French.

Jared smiled. "Whoa, ladies. I don't understand French."

Brigit blew him a kiss. "I said that I want to kiss you."

"We both do," Renee said. "There can be no one else behind these murders. We are *both* flying to Canada to question Jasmine and Victoria Fontaine. We suspect that the daughter has no idea of her lineage, but the mother certainly does."

"Have you watched the interview?" Jared asked.

"We have yet to finish it."

"I haven't seen the whole thing either. But there was more than one reason he didn't want his daughter digging into her genealogy."

"Indeed. Michelle Le Claire abandoned two daughters. It should not surprise us. Mon ami, I want you to question Jasmine Fontaine. We will make arrangements for you to do it from there."

"Thank you. I watch these interviews and think of follow-up questions I would have asked. It will be nice to have that opportunity."

"You have earned it. If we are able to capture Michelle Le Claire, you can expect a commendation."

"I don't expect that. I just want justice for Henri."

"And for all the others that woman murdered."

Chapter 20

Jared finished viewing the Victoria Fontaine interview, more interested in watching Jasmine's reaction than listening to the daughter's answers. Neither provided much information.

Philippe had offered his daughter a tearful apology for all the revelations she had heard and would hear about him. He reminded her that he loved her. Those were the last words he said to her. Jasmine remained passive throughout the interview, simply holding her step-daughter's hand.

Jared saw a mother's unconditional love. He stood and stretched.

Rita spoke. "Incoming message from Dr. Mason-Pearce. 'Are you coming home?'"

Jared chuckled. "Connect me."

Karen's voice came in his ear. "Developments?"

"Yeah. Big time. Let's go out to supper."

"I'll have my clothes changed by the time you get here."

Jared jogged home. Karen handed him a glass of wine when he entered.

"It sounded like you have cause for celebration."

"We know who killed Henri." He swirled the wine. "Kind of an ironic way to celebrate."

"That wasn't lost on me, either. Well?"

"The ex-wife, who we thought was long-dead. And her boyfriend created the poison."

"Wow. If everybody thinks she's dead, how did you decide that she poisoned him?"

Jared sipped wine, then removed his weapon belt. "She started crossing my mind awhile ago. Today, I ran facial comparison on a woman born after she supposedly died. Rita said they are mother and daughter."

"And she couldn't have been the result of a frozen embryo?"

"Don't rain on my parade." He raised an eyebrow, then smiled. "Possible. Not probable. The CV compound didn't have that kind of medical facilities. No, Michelle Le Claire survived the crackdown. I spoke to a retired cop today who always believed that she had."

"Great police work." Karen kissed him.

"Um-m. We'd better go out to supper before I think of other ways to celebrate."

Karen traced his lips with her fingertip. "We'll get to that. I'm guessing you still have to find the cold-blooded witch."

"Don't remind me. I keep telling myself that until today no one was searching for her. Now she'll be on top of the most wanted list of every law enforcement agency on the planet."

***

Jared paced outside his office, waiting for Renee to set up the interview. *No room for pacing inside.*

Renee and Brigit had taken the red eye flight to Montreal. The interview was set for 1:00 PM local time, five hours behind his Zulu time. He had told Karen not to wait on him for supper.

"Connection in progress," Rita said in his ear.

Jared entered the office and took a seat behind the desk.

Jasmine Fontaine's image appeared, this time in an interrogation room. He heard Renee's voice.

"Madam Fontaine, this is Inspector Pearce, Chief of Lunar Enforcement. He will be conducting this interview."

"Why?"

"That will become evident. Inspector Pearce."

Jared took a deep breath. "Mrs. Fontaine, I know this is a difficult time for you. But this is very important. I need you to tell me about how you met your husband."

Fontaine frowned, but nodded. "It was at university. I was sitting alone in the cafeteria and he asked to join me. He said that I looked like I needed a friend, and I did." She wiped her eyes. "I had just received depressing medical news. He was a godsend."

"How long was your courtship?"

She smiled. "Only three months. In less than two weeks, he earned my trust. We became inseparable. When he began to speak of marriage, I told him the depressing news. Though I had viable eggs, I could not maintain a pregnancy. That did not deter him. He said that we would simply hire a surrogate. How could I not love such a man?"

"That would certainly win your heart. Was Victoria your first child?"

"Yes. He did not want to wait until we graduated. I worried about the cost. However, he had a small inheritance. He researched everything. Two months after our marriage, we went to the clinic. A month later, he told me that the surrogate was pregnant."

"Did you meet her?"

"No. She wanted to remain anonymous. The surrogates for our other two children chose not to. Why is this important?"

Jared debated for a moment. *She's clueless. But I can't afford to let her keep living in this fantasy world. We need information.* "We believe your husband knew Victoria's surrogate."

"What? What are you saying? That my husband had a child with this woman and passed her off as my daughter?"

"That's exactly what I'm saying. We used facial recognition. Victoria is *not* your biological daughter."

Jasmine Fontaine's expression showed outrage, then disbelief. Then she sagged in her chair. "She just looks more like Philippe."

"That's what you've told yourself all these years. Your husband wasn't a handsome man. Victoria is stunning. She looks like her biological mother."

Jasmine nodded and wiped her eyes. "When our son was born, I saw the difference. But Philippe was such a loving husband, I could not believe that he would be unfaithful. I convinced myself that there must have been an error at the clinic. I told him that."

"What did he say?"

"He studied the children and concurred with my assessment. He suggested that they fertilized my egg with the wrong sperm. He said that we had the basis for a lawsuit, but he loved Victoria no matter who her parents were. He did not want to risk losing her to a biological parent. I agreed and we never discussed it again."

"Her mother was a woman he knew from the *Cause Vertueuse*. They had about a nine-year relationship before he moved to Canada. She must have joined him after the crackdown."

"Then why did he marry me? Why not marry that woman?"

"We don't know."

"Is she still here? Did he continue this affair all this time?"

"We think she left Montreal. But they stayed in contact. He created the poison for her. Over the years, did he do anything to make you suspicious."

"Was her name Michelle?"

"Yes, why?"

"Before we were married, he called me Michelle once. He apologized and said it was the name of an old girlfriend." She sighed. "When Victoria was a few months old, I noticed a woman watching us in the park. I wondered if she was the surrogate."

"Did you speak to her?"

"When I approached her, she walked away."

"Do you remember what she looked like?"

"She was lovely. But she did not look like Victoria."

Jared clenched his fists. "Hair color? Eye color? Height? Weight? Distinguishing features?"

Jasmine's brow furrowed and she squeezed the bridge of her nose. "Blonde." She dropped her hand. "Nicely tanned. I could not see her eyes. Tall ... about Victoria's height. A symmetrical face. Nothing prominent. She appeared in good condition. Not fat or thin."

An average good-looking woman. Useful. "Did you ever see her again?"

"No."

"Again, did your husband do anything to make you suspicious?"

"No. Oh, I worried when he traveled for business. But when he came home, he brought me gifts and he showed me how much he missed me. My husband loved me. If he maintained a relationship with this woman, I forgive him. Have you considered that she may have blackmailed him with knowledge of his past?"

"We're not ruling anything out. Did he say anything to you after his arrest?"

"I already spoke to the RCMP about this. He apologized for the revelations and told me that he loved me. He asked me to remember the happy times."

"Thank you, Mrs. Fontaine. That's all I have. Captain Julian."

"Thank you, Inspector. Madam, did you ever tell Victoria about your suspicions concerning her parentage?"

"No. Please, do not tell her."

"I am afraid that is inevitable. She also has a sister in France she deserves to know about."

Jasmine wiped her eyes again. "Please let me be the one to tell her."

"You have until tomorrow. After that, I make no guarantees. That will be all for now. Inspector Pearce, I will speak to you momentarily."

The image vanished.

Jared stomach growled. "Rita, I'm going to grab something to eat."

***

Rita's voice came in his ear as he returned from the cafeteria. "Incoming call from Captain Julian."

"Put her through. Sorry, Renee, I won't have video for a minute. It's past my suppertime."

Renee chuckled. "Ours also. We obtained sandwiches before I made this call. We will have a dinner meeting."

Jared entered the office. "I'm not sure that Mrs. Fontaine provided anything useful." Renee and Brigit appeared on his wall.

"True. I know a dozen women who fit her description. And hair color is no more than a whim."

"Right." Jared used chopsticks on chicken and broccoli. "We could dig into his business travel. He may have used the trips to rendevous with Michelle Le Claire."

"It will be done. Though it is not as simple as connecting two known persons, we may find something."

"I think he targeted Jasmine. It can't be coincidence that he picked a woman who couldn't carry a child. Somehow, they got hold of her medical records."

"Indeed. What is your opinion on why he married her, not Michelle Le Claire?"

"It's obvious that he was totally devoted to Michelle. He created the poison, then killed himself rather than risk betraying her. He married Jasmine because Michelle told him to."

Brigit spoke with her mouth full. "Why?"

"I don't think Michelle has ever loved anyone. She left two daughters. I think even they were pawns to get what she wants. She had a child with Henri to keep him in the CV. That backfired on her. She probably told Philippe that it was too dangerous for them to stay together. If she had just left, she might not have been able to count on him for future assistance."

"So she left him with a child."

Renee nodded. "By posing as a surrogate. No one would ask him questions about the mother of his child."

"We always knew that she was the mastermind." Brigit's frown deepened. "CV attacks were much better planned after she came of age."

Jared sighed. "It's no wonder she's been able to evade capture for more than thirty years."

"But it would seem that with all the DNA testing, she would have been found out."

"Not necessarily. With the exception of law enforcement, military, and sensitive positions, DNA isn't collected. It's turned in."

"No. How can this be?"

"Let's say someone is traveling. Their DNA has to be on record in case of an accident. Because of our jobs, we're already in the database. Let's say the traveler is a waitress. She's never been tested. She picks up a swab at her local pharmacy, takes her own test, and turns it in. The pharmacy adds her picture and she's in the database."

"All Le Claire had to do was have someone else provide a sample?"

"Someone who wasn't already in the database. The last estimate I saw was that around twenty-five percent of people aren't. Most of those are in second world countries. First world countries, the estimate is more like ten percent."

"I was not aware. That is a horrible flaw in the system."

"The vast majority of people will provide an accurate sample. But it does allow wanted criminals like Michelle Le Claire to go undetected. Her doctor would have her actual DNA on file, but medical facilities don't access the database and aren't allowed to share records without a court order."

"If we find a viable suspect," Renee said. "We can get that court order."

"I hope the computers find a clue in Fontaine's travel history."

"Indeed. Well, mon ami, we are very tired. We will talk to Victoria Fontaine tomorrow before returning to France. I do not expect anything useful from the interview, but you will receive a video nonetheless."

"Thanks, Renee. I'll talk to you tomorrow."

Chapter 21

When Jared watched the Victoria Fontaine interview, she seemed almost shell-shocked by the revelation about her biological mother. She had no memory of meeting a woman who might have been Michelle Le Claire.

Philippe Fontaine's travel records provided intriguing evidence which brought them no closer to finding the fugitive. During decade-old business stays in New York, Chicago, Phoenix, and Vancouver, he had added a second person to his room at check-in. However, Jasmine Fontaine had not made the trip.

The stays had occurred so long ago that hotel security video had been erased.

Either the pair became more discreet after that or the affair ended.

Jared leaned back in his chair. *It would be a simple matter for them to get separate rooms on the same floor. I'm sure the computer is checking video of more recent trips.*

"Chief," Rita said. "Breach drill in one hour."

"Thanks, Rita." Jared jumped up from his chair and left the office. Lars leaned against the wall outside as Halolani approached.

Marek arrived a moment later, with Rudy bringing up the rear. Jared smiled at Marek. "The rest know this without being told. An hour from now, we're having a surprise breach drill."

Some of the color left Marek's face and he swallowed hard. "Thank God we didn't have it a month ago. Who else knows?"

"Just us and Environmental Control. The head of EC and I picked the time. EC personnel were notified at the same time I told you. I assume you reviewed protocols."

"I can recite them for you." Marek smiled. "I committed that one to memory."

"Good. There will be EC staff in every pod. We will work with them to move everyone to secure locations. Marek, what's the first thing that happens in the event of a breach?"

"Doors around the breach close, followed by doors between the pods."

"I'm assigning you to the hub. Where is the safe location for people there?"

"Any of the spokes."

"Good. How long do you stay there?"

"Until the all-clear is given or someone comes to escort us out."

Jared smiled. "And if an actual breach happened when you were at home?"

"Shelter in place. Take our space suits out of their cases."

"Let's give Officer Dorshak a round of applause." The other LEOs clapped. Jared continued. "Lars, take temporary housing,

Halolani, the school, Rudy, singles. I'll take the farm. EC can handle corporate. After all clear, we'll meet at the corporate cafeteria for debriefing. Marek, take your time getting to the hub. Arrive no more than five minutes before the alarm. It's hard to look like you're just patrolling in the dome for any longer than that." He checked his watch. "T minus forty-eight minutes. Let's go."

The officers scattered. Jared strolled to his home pod, then circled the walkway around the farm, greeting people as he would any other day. He entered the farm. *Everyone is used to seeing me here. They won't think anything of it.* He talked to the workers and pretended to admire the crops.

The alarm sounded and the computer gave instructions. "This is a drill. Breach in the school pod. This is a drill. Go to the nearest secure location. This is a drill ..." The alarm and warning continued.

Farm workers dropped what they were doing and ran for the walkway. Jared followed. Those who lived in the pod entered their apartments. Two others chose the barber shop. Jared found a wide-eyed woman, frozen in place.

"Go in the bank."

He had to take her shoulders and turn her before she moved in that direction. After a quick look around, he returned to the bank, where a female employee sat holding her hand. Caroline Delhomme occupied another chair.

Jared smiled. "How are you doing, Dr. Wyndham-Jones?"

She let her breath out. "Better. I apologize for the hysteria, Chief. I fear that I have yet to feel comfortable here."

"I understand. I went through the same thing. Breach drills here are like fire drills on Earth. We need to be prepared. But there has never been a breach. At any of the settlements."

"They told us during orientation. Yet, when the alarm sounded, I forgot everything. It is reassuring to know that even a man's man like you took time to adjust."

Jared chuckled. "I was terrified. How are you doing, Ms. Delhomme?"

"Will you feel badly if I say I was merely startled by the alarm?"

"No. You won't bruise my ego. At least half the people come to the moon because they really want to. They're excited about it. You said you came because you wanted a new adventure. Breach drills are part of the adventure."

"I preferred climbing mountains. However, a knee injury put an end to that. How difficult is it to obtain permission to go out and walk on the surface?"

"Contact parks and recreation. They have regularly scheduled moon walks. Numbers are limited, but they aren't really that popular. The novelty wears off for a lot of people."

The bank employee stood. "Can I get any of you some coffee or tea?"

"Espresso," Delhomme said.

Dr. Wyndham-Jones looked from the employee to Jared. "How long will we be here?"

Jared checked his watch. "Probably another twenty minutes. EC has a list of protocols to go through before the all-clear. I'll have a cup of coffee. Hazelnut."

"Earl Grey tea would be lovely, thank you." The employee left the lobby. "How often do we have these drills?"

"Quarterly."

"I shall do better during the next one." Her eyes widened. "I wonder how the children handled this?"

"They're fine. The school is a shelter-in-place location. And they hold drills monthly. So your kids have been through one already."

"That's right. They mentioned it. You are a very calming influence, Chief."

He smiled. "That means I'm doing my job. We're less of a crime solving force and more of a public relations unit."

Delhomme snorted. "Until someone is murdered."

"That's true. We're totally capable of investigating crimes."

***

Even computers took some time to review hotel security video from hundreds of hotels and thousands of stays. Renee did not call Jared with results for another week.

"She is a sly one, mon ami."

"But you got pictures of her?"

"Useless pictures. Fontaine was seeing a blonde woman, approximately one-point-seven-five meters tall, of average build. We assume it is Michelle Le Claire."

"How often was she spotted?"

"Only three times. In Seattle, New York, and Miami."

"When was the most recent?"

"A year ago in Miami."

Jared leaned back in his chair. "So we're no closer to catching her than we were before."

"That lead has brought us no closer. However, we do have a slim lead from London."

Jared straightened. "The courier company."

"Yes. The sender met the courier in the lobby of an apartment. The address he gave was false. However, the apartment's security cameras caught images of him. Even with the disguise he wore, the computer has generated a likeness with a high probability of accuracy. It is running facial recognition now."

"That *is* good news. If we can capture him alive, hopefully he won't be as loyal to Michelle as Fontaine was."

"And he may know where to find her."

"Amen. I have a question for you. Should I tell Rachelle Le Claire that her mother is alive? And a secondary question. That she has a half-sister?"

"I have been considering the same questions. Yes. And it is best that the information comes from you. Every law enforcement agency in the world is searching for her mother. As yet, that information has not been made public. However, it is just a matter of time before the news spreads. Use your discretion concerning the half-sister."

"I think after finding out her mother is alive, knowing that she also abandoned another child may be a comfort to her. She'll be less likely to blame herself."

"Ah-h. Well said. I do not envy you that task."

"It has to be better than telling her Henri was murdered."

"Indeed. I will call if the computer matches the sketch."

"Thank, Renee. Rita, end call. Send a message to Rachelle Le Clair."

"Go ahead, Chief."

"Call me when you get off work. End message. That's not something she needs to deal with at work."

"Message sent. You have a message from Dr. Mason-Pearce. 'Don't forget Allison's art showing.' End message."

Jared smiled. "She knows me so well."

Chapter 22

Jared was at home, changing, when Rita told him that he had a call from Rachelle. He took a seat in front of the camera.

"Go ahead."

Rachelle appeared, sitting in her car. "You have news, Chief."

"Yes. Tough news. I was hoping you would call me from home."

"Do not be concerned." She took a deep breath, then let it out. "Tell me."

"You were right as a child. Your mother is alive."

Rachelle covered her mouth for a moment. "But she never tried to see me. She could have made arrangements. Family would have protected her. Are you certain?"

"Yes. To answer your next question, we still have no idea where she is. Probably the US or Canada."

"How did you find her then?"

"I began to suspect that you were right. When we found Philippe Fontaine, he had a daughter who looks much like you. She's about twelve years younger. Facial recognition tells us that you have the same mother."

Tears began running down Rachelle's cheeks. "Did Maman abandon her too?"

"Yes."

"How could she do that? Is she *so* horrible?"

"I won't badmouth your mother. I'm sure you have good memories of her. I'm sorry I have to be the one to tell you this."

"I once had good memories of her." She wiped tears and her face hardened. "They were fantasies. Maman enjoyed having me entertain her, but the love I knew came from Grand-mère. Maman never wanted me to hug her. I was allowed to kiss her cheek ... Is Maman responsible for Papa's death?"

"We believe so. Philippe created the poison, but he had no reason to want your father dead."

"Do you think she did it because I had begun a relationship with Papa?"

"No. No, I don't think that had anything to do with it. I believe that she is about to do something that will put her in the public eye. Even with cosmetic surgery, those who knew her best could still recognize her. People like Henri."

"But I knew her better than almost anyone. She has not tried to kill me."

"You knew her with a child's eyes. After all these years, you're less likely to recognize her. I don't believe you're in any danger."

Karen entered the apartment, realized that he was working, then walked behind Jared to the bedroom.

Rachelle saw her. "You are at home, Chief. I should not take any more of your time."

"We can take all the time we need. I want to make sure you're okay to drive home."

"Thank you, Chief. I will put the car in self-driving mode. I will talk to my husband on the way. May I contact my sister?"

"I'll suggest that you send her a message to contact you when she's ready. She not only lost her father, but she also found out that her mother isn't her biological mother. I'll send you the information though."

"Thank you, Chief. I will go now. Au revoir."

"Goodbye, Rachelle. Rita, end call." He joined Karen in the bedroom. "That was a tough one."

"You had to tell Rachelle that her mother abandoned her."

"Yeah." He slipped on the jacket to his dress uniform. "She's known for a long time that her mother never loved her. She just couldn't admit it to herself."

"The children were just pawns to Michelle?"

Jared nodded. "Things she could use to get what she wanted. I need this evening of mindless chitchat to unwind."

"I'm sure Allison would appreciate you referring to her art showing in that context." Karen laughed.

"She will never know. I'll also enjoy seeing her art in person."

"Zip my dress." She turned her back to him. "The school kids went to the art show this afternoon. Lloyd said they loved it and asked all kinds of questions. Did you know she's terra formed with one of her molds?"

"I hadn't heard that."

"She started out simple, an eagle's head. It worked."

"Great. I'd like to see her selling to tourists. She can probably make more here than in any of the galleries she had on Earth. Are we ready?"

"As soon as I get my necklace and earrings."

***

Allison and Lloyd greeted everyone at the door to the multi-purpose room. Lloyd wore a tuxedo for the occasion and Allison a loose, flowing gown in a peacock feather pattern.

Allison beamed when she saw them. "Oh, thank you both for coming. You're two of the few people I know by name."

Karen chuckled. "This will go a long way toward getting to know more. Everyone I talked to was excited about this."

"That is wonderful. Have a glass of wine and hors d'oeuvres. Enjoy my art."

Jared procured glasses from a waiter, then he and Karen circled the makeshift gallery. Allison sculpted mostly birds of prey—eagles, falcons, hawks, and owls. Only one casting featured wolves, though Jared had seen more on her website.

The exhibit included a half-dozen copies of the eagle's head. She had left one the color of the regolith, another had been bronzed, two more gilded, and the last two treated to look like marble.

"Impressive." Jared finished his wine. "If I didn't know what they were made of, I'd never guess."

"They will fly off the shelves if she can get a shop at Lunar Adventures. Let's grab some hors d'oeuvres. I'm starving."

"Right behind you."

Food service had prepared a wide assortment of delicacies, some local, others imported from Earth. Jared and Karen satisfied their hunger, then she chose another glass of wine while he switched to Aqua Luna sparkling water.

Karen smiled. "Always on duty."

"I'm in uniform, so yeah."

"And it's just coincidence that you don't own a suit. The only thing you have to wear at formal occasions is your dress uniform."

"No, it's because I'm a tightwad." He chuckled.

"You're full of it, Chief. Let's look at her sketches."

Karen had described the two-dimensional art as just good. Jared shook his head. *They look great to me.* He lingered at each one while Karen moved on. He ended up next to Marguerite Boyle.

"What do you think of it?" Jared asked.

"I am jealous. Do you remember from my file, my college degrees?"

Jared pursed his lips. "Yeah. Well, not exactly. Something to do with art."

"Very good. Art history. Museum management. I studied water color in Paris. And I am working in the shipping department of a mining company."

"So, you're a frustrated artist."

"I was a very poor artist. That led to frustration and a career change. Working for a gallery or museum was too difficult." She finished her wine. "Ah, well. I long ago reconciled myself to reality. Had I stayed in the field, I never would have had the opportunity to live here."

"Attitude is a big part of happiness. You've just answered a question for me. You never quite sounded like someone from Maine. The time in Paris explains that."

"Oui. Je parlais Français couramment." She smiled. "And to answer what I—an educated art lover—think, Mrs. Desjarlais's sculpture is excellent. Her charcoals and pastels are better than I could have done. Excuse me. I need a refill."

She drifted away and Jared moved on to a charcoal drawing of great horned owls.

"I am embarrassed to include them in a show," Allison said at his elbow.

"The owls?"

"All the charcoals and pastels. They simply were easier to ship than more sculptures."

"Don't be embarrassed. They may not meet your standards. But they're pretty impressive to the average ignorant art lover like me."

Allison chuckled. "You say that. But Lloyd tells me that one of the cases in your previous job involved international art theft."

Jared raised his eyebrows. "Lloyd really does his research."

"Only on people whom he finds challenging. He has been in a command position for many years. People defer to him. When someone doesn't, he is intrigued."

"So I'm both challenging and intriguing." He smiled. "I've been called worse."

"His research has led to admiration. I trust his judgement. You surely learned something about art from that case."

"Yes, I did. Crew members on a carrier stole art when the carrier was in port, then smuggled it out on board. I learned a lot about museum security. I learned what makes a piece valuable, no matter the school. The works they stole were very valuable, but not really my taste. That was the first case I worked with Interpol."

"And what *is* your taste in art?"

"Your work. Realism. Animals. Landscapes. Nature. I think your art is especially important here, because we can't see it out our window."

Allison placed her palm to her chest and her eyes glistened. "Thank you." She took a deep breath, then smiled. "You call yourself an ignorant art lover. I think not."

***

"Pabaiga?" Jared repeated.

Renee nodded. "It is Lithuanian for 'the end.' We have no knowledge of his real name. He is a murderer for hire. He has killed many ways, including 'sub-contracting' hits to other killers."

"He hired Lange."

"Oui. He uses a variety of disguises, but computers have recognized him in multiple places around the globe when murders occurred."

"Any of our murders?"

"Two. But the computers are still working. Because we are dealing with poison, we begin with the approximate date the victims started showing symptoms. It is a slow process."

"I don't know if that's even important. We know he's the accomplice. He's been getting away with murder for years. None of the law enforcement organizations in the world have been able to find him. How will we?"

"Indeed. There is the problem, mon ami. I will send you the collection of other murders and leads to his whereabouts. Put your mind to it. Sending now."

"It will give me something to do. By the way, I haven't heard an update on the survivors lately. How are they doing?"

"All are symptom free, with the exception of one. He was in critical condition for some time, but is now home with supplemental oxygen."

"That's good. The file is here. I guess I'll get to work on it." Jared disconnected. "Rita, show me the cases in chronological order, without the conclusions or theories of the investigating agencies."

Jared studied each file, taking notes with an old-fashioned pen and paper. Pabaiga had no preferred murder method. And no concern for collateral damage. If his target lived in an apartment building, arson was still an option. Jared gritted his teeth as he read the account of nine people killed to eliminate one.

He took a deep breath, then let it out before moving on to the next case. Hours passed. His notes piled up.

"Chief," Rita said. "It's past your lunchtime."

"I know."

Rita said no more. A half-hour later, the door opened and Lars entered.

Jared leaned back in his chair and stretched. "What's up?"

"Three people mentioned that they had not seen the chief today. I thought I should check."

Jared stood, then rubbed his back. "Interpol identified the accomplice, an international hit man known as Pabaiga."

"Is that Lithuanian?"

"Yes. It means the end. I'm going through all the cases tied to him."

Lars took a seat. "Tell me what you have."

"He kills indiscriminately. He's credited with shooting, stabbing, poisoning, arson, hit-and-run, drowning, beating, and throwing people from buildings. He's struck mostly in the Northern Hemisphere, but he's killed on every continent, including Antarctica. That victim died of exposure."

"And he struck here."

"Yeah." Jared settled into his chair again.

"How can I help?"

Jared chuckled. "Would you get me some lunch?"

"Certainly. But would your body benefit from the exercise?"

"Of course it would."

"I will walk to the cafeteria with you."

"I'm coming. I'm coming."

***

Jared spent three days combing through the Pabaiga files. He waited until reaching his own conclusions before surveying those from the investigating agencies, then called Renee to report his findings.

"Tell me you have discovered something, mon ami."

"Maybe. Most of my conclusions agree with what's in the files. But there's one aberration. A man was killed in Austria four years ago—a groundskeeper who had lived his whole life in Salzburg. Investigators never found any record of a hit on him or any reason for one. He wasn't collateral damage from another hit. Pabaiga didn't kill anyone else in Salzburg."

"Therefore, the victim did not witness another of his murders. Do you think Pabaiga may have lived in Salzburg?"

"It's plausible. The victim worked in a gated community. He was run down with a stolen car in another part of town. Witnesses said that the driver accelerated toward him, so it wasn't an accident. Investigators spoke to residents of the gated community. I didn't have access to the videos of those interviews. I'd like to see pictures of the residents."

"You will have them. I will instruct the computer to compare them to the likeness of Pabaiga. And I will pass this information on to our inspectors in Austria."

"I hope it helps."

"As do I. On a different subject, I have been asked to send you another case file to review. The inspectors working the case do not know how to proceed. Perhaps you can assist them."

Jared smiled. "I get to start earning my paycheck."

"Paycheck?" Renee laughed. "How old *are* you?"

"You know how old I am. What can I say? I grew up in a rural area. People still wrote checks."

"I found them when I cleaned out my parents home, but I had never written or received one. A relic from the past."

"I'm kind of a relic myself. Send me the file. I'll get to work."
***

Jared spent the rest of the day reviewing the case. The next morning he rose early and called the inspectors with suggestions. He disconnected and smiled.

That felt good. He had contributed to the investigation and may have helped solve a crime. *It doesn't make up for the frustration of not catching Henri's killer, but it helps.*

Karen came from the bedroom. "You're up early." She kissed him. "Happy Birthday."

"Thank you. I had to call Interpol in Delhi with my report."

"What are your plans for today?"

"I thought I'd go fishing." He laughed.

"You could probably arrange that. Though it wouldn't be much of a challenge."

"No. I *am* going fishing when we're in Colorado for Joel's wedding."

"Only if you take me along."

Jared pulled her into his lap. "Deal. I'm just planning to work today. I'll knock off a little early to change for our night out."

"Knock off about three and we'll do a little celebrating before we go out."

He grinned. "Sounds like my kind of celebration."

She leaned close and blew in his ear. "That will be the encore. This is the first act."

Jared stood and carried her into the bedroom.

***

Jared met Halolani on the way to his office.

"Happy Birthday, Chief. Kind of late to work this morning. You must have been opening presents."

Jared gave her a sweet smile. "Walk with me. Anything to report?"

"Nothing. Same as every other day."

"You're one of my youngest officers. Do you ever get bored?"

"What's being under forty have to do with boredom?"

Jared shrugged. "Us old people have had enough excitement for a lifetime."

"The answer is no. I had too much excitement for a lifetime. Do you remember what I told you when you interviewed me?"

"That you'd seen too many bodies. You liked police work, but you didn't want to see more bodies and you didn't want to sit behind a desk either."

"That still applies. Here, I get all the feel good stuff that goes with being a cop and none of the negativity. This place is like Mayberry."

He laughed. "I haven't heard that comparison in a long time. It's a pretty good one. But I'm kind of surprised you know about Mayberry."

"My parents liked the show. There's no town on Earth where you can force troublemakers to leave, no matter who they are." She slapped his back. "I know you wouldn't take the job without that rule in place. Thanks for giving us that power."

"So that's it. You're on a power trip."

"I'm just a tyrant." She giggled.

Rita's voice came in Jared's ear. "Mayor Carlson requests your presence at the school. She had to break up a fight between two eighth-grade boys."

"We're on our way." He changed directions and Halolani followed. "This should be interesting. A fight at school."

"Only the second one, ever. There's another example of why I like it here. We have so little crime that we handle discipline for the school."

"Just the serious stuff."

They made quick work of the distance. Through the glass doors, Jared saw students at their lockers or standing around visiting.

The doors slid open as he and Halolani approached. Everyone inside turned their way.

"Surprise!" Came from a chorus of voices. The scrolling sign around the top of the common area began displaying "Happy Birthday, Chief."

Jared stopped in his tracks. Halolani laughed and the students gathered around him with birthday wishes.

He mumbled thanks before adjusting to the new development. "This is a big disappointment. I was all prepared to give someone a lecture about fighting."

The kids laughed. Adults joined the crowd, including Angela Carlson and Karen.

Karen slipped through to his side and kissed his cheek. "Surprised you, didn't we."

"Yes. Does everyone know about this?"

"Pretty much."

"Mayor Carlson, there's a little matter of filing a false report."

Angela raised her eyebrows. "I didn't sign anything."

"Well, Rita didn't lie to me. If you told her there was a fight, that's as good as a signature." He laughed.

Jared spent the next hour visiting with party-goers and eating carrot cake with cream cheese frosting, his favorite.

Lloyd whistled to silence the crowd. "Now, Chief Pearce, what's a party without a gift?" He patted a wrapped box sitting on the podium next to him. "Almost everyone in the settlement chipped in for this, including the kids." He glanced at his wife. "Plus we got a really good deal on it. Come over here and take a look."

Jared approached, shaking his head. "How do I open that thing?"

"Just lift the box off."

Jared followed instructions, revealing a foot-tall bronze casting of Allison's eagle catching a fish. His jaw dropped. "Wow!"

The crowd applauded. Allison's booming laugh rose above the noise.

Jared met her gaze. "Thank you."

She approached and gave him a hug. "You said it was your favorite. The original is much larger. But this is a limited edition. Only five hundred of this size were cast."

"I love it. What was the title again?"

"Catch of the Day."

"Thank you."

"Speech," Lloyd said.

Several people repeated it and the crowd quieted.

Jared cleared his throat. "Congratulations on pulling off the biggest caper in Tranquility history. I should really resign because, as police chief, I should have caught on to your plan." People laughed. "But, obviously, all of my officers were in on the conspiracy, so I can be forgiven." More chuckles. "Thank you, all. It's been a great party. The gift is ... I have no words. You answered the question, 'What do you get for the man who has everything?' Thank you, so much."

The crowd applauded, then began to disburse. Jared delivered personal thanks to a number of people before he and Karen headed back to their apartment with his gift.

He squeezed her hand. "You're devious."

"You've known that for a long time. You must have known there would be some kind of party. We weren't going to let a milestone birthday pass without one."

"I thought that's what you really had planned for three o'clock. Probably you and my officers. Maybe a few close friends. Nothing like this."

"This was the students' idea. When they saw your name on the birthday schedule, they asked their teachers if they could have a party for you. It ballooned from there."

"It might be my most memorable birthday ever."

Chapter 23

Weeks passed with no progress in the CV killer case. Pabaiga continued to evade detection. Jared consulted on an Interpol case almost every-other-week and found satisfaction in that part of his job.

As their vacation approached, he and Karen prepared by wearing Earth vests, adding five hundred pounds of Earth weight. The vests cut the time to adjust to Earth's gravity from two weeks to a few days.

The day before his departure, Jared sat down to lunch with his Tranquility officers. Lars had retired, leaving Halolani his second in command. Rudy, Marek, and Ty completed the team.

"Marek, you're the only one who hasn't been through this before. But by now you know the chances of anything happening that the four of you can't handle are pretty remote. Still, I'm just a call away. We'll be spending most of our vacation in the US Mountain Daylight Time zone, so don't call me too early." He smiled.

Halolani shook her head. "You'll be the one calling us, if this vacation is anything like the last three."

"Probably. But I have a lot more going on this time. Besides the wedding, I have to meet with my superiors at Interpol before I come back. And see Henri's daughter."

"You'll really be globetrotting on this trip."

Ty chuckled. "Say hi to Texas when you're in Houston."

"We don't plan to be there long," Jared said. "The twenty-four hour hold for our physicals, then we fly to Santa Fe. We'll be on our ranch in seventy-two hours."

"Ride a horse for me too."

"Haven't you heard? You'll be able to do that here soon."

Ty stared. "Don't mess with me, Chief."

"They're preparing the room now. The robot mimics the feel of a horse's movements. It looks like a horse, even has hair. You can pick the breed, which controls how high it carries its head and picks up its feet. You can put different saddles on it. The room is a holographic projector to let you pick where you ride. There are fans. The faster you ride, the stronger the wind. There will be two horse robots, so you don't have to ride alone."

Ty emitted a loud whistle. "I may never retire."

"It should be installed by the time I get back. I have a feeling it will be pretty popular."

"Do they have a sign-up sheet yet?"

"Talk to parks and recreation. Well, I'd better get back to the office and finish my paperwork. Our rover leaves first thing in the morning and I still have to pack."

***

When the rover bus arrived at Apennine, the passengers returning to Earth entered an airlock leading to the "dark side." The settlement's Lunar Enforcement officers met Jared and Karen. After greeting them, Karen retired to their hotel room. Jared patrolled with his newest officer, Omar Naseem from Kuwait.

That evening, they all dined at *The Round Table* with Phyllis sitting alone on the "light side." Karen had been a law enforcement wife for so long that she could talk shop with the officers.

She and Jared turned in early, since their interplanetary ship left at 0600. That meant arriving at 0400 to get strapped into their space suits.

The spacecraft lifted off right on time. During the ten hour flight, Jared visited with Karen, watched two movies, and ate the in-flight food pouches. That still left plenty of time for stargazing.

The ship docked at Shepard Spaceport at 1545 hours.

Jared grinned. "We must have caught a tailwind." He unbuckled his harness.

"Funny man." Karen rolled her eyes.

A hatch opened and a spaceport crewman floated in. "Okay, folks. Everybody free? Follow me to the Earth shuttle."

They floated down a tunnel using hand rails on the walls to pull themselves along. The crewman stopped by another hatch where the travelers entered a more cramped version of the interplanetary ship.

After all the passengers had chosen a seat, the crewman floated in to assist anyone who needed help with their harness. He talked as he worked.

"If any of you will be experiencing your first reentry, you're in for an amazing light show."

Jared managed to get his harness buckled. *Don't remind me.* He was now considered a seasoned space traveler, but reentry still made him nervous. *Yeah, no shuttle has burned up since the* Columbia. *It's still the most dangerous part of the trip.* He saw Karen change her com to private mode and did the same.

She smiled. "This part still makes me nervous."

"You're reading my mind. You'd think they could design a spacecraft that would ease into the atmosphere without the friction."

"I heard that they did, but it was too expensive to operate."

"That figures. I suppose we'd better open our coms so we can hear commands."

Within minutes, the crewman closed the hatch and strapped himself into a seat. The shuttle separated and moved to a lower orbit, circling the Earth twice while the pilots prepared for reentry.

The ride started to get bumpy and a glow appeared outside the windows. The situation deteriorated before the flames disappeared and the blackness of space morphed into the blue sky of Earth.

A screen at the front of the cabin showed everyone what lay below. The Pacific Ocean gave way to Baja California, the Sea of Cortez, then Mexico. As the craft descended, Jared started to recognize cities.

The shuttle made a perfect landing at the Johnson Space Center. When it came to a stop, the crewman levered himself from his seat and opened the hatch. Passengers started unbuckling, but did not try to rise.

From his window, Jared saw the ground vehicle approach. It looked like a shipping container on wheels. The driver stood at controls in an accordion tunnel. When it reached the shuttle, she raised the vehicle to hatch level and extended the tunnel.

Two ground crew members entered and began helping the passengers stand one at a time. Another steadied them as they walked from the shuttle. Jared felt like he weighed a thousand pounds.

When he entered the ground vehicle, a woman removed his helmet. "Welcome to Houston."

"I recognize the humidity."

"A common complaint after your climate-controlled environment." She placed the helmet on a rack, then removed his gloves. "Have you been wearing the Earth vest?"

"Yeah. For the better part of a month."

"Good. You've been through this before, haven't you." She circled to his back to free him from his suit.

"This is my fourth reentry."

"Then I don't have to tell you what to expect." She returned to a position facing him, then pulled the suit off his arms first, then all the way down to his legs.

Jared settled into a cushioned chair opposite the rack before she removed his boots, then the rest of the suit. "Thanks."

Karen occupied the seat next to him. "I'm tired already."

"Whoever decided that a nap should be the first thing on our schedule was a genius."

***

Jared slept for three hours, his vital signs checked by medical personnel through a monitor around his wrist. He woke in the white room with its twin air beds and pried himself to a sitting position.

This really makes me feel old. Everything required effort and slow movement. He shuffled to the bathroom, showered, and found surgical scrubs in a cabinet there. He left the room without waking Karen.

A man in a NASA lab coat met him outside. "Mr. Pearce, how are you feeling?"

"About what you'd expect."

"Which is?"

"Old. Tired. No different than the last three times I made this trip."

"Good. Be sure to let us know if you experience anything you haven't before. Come with me. We'll get you something to eat."

Jared followed him to a dining room with soft arm chairs. Everything in this facility was designed for the comfort of people adjusting to gravity. Only one other person occupied a table.

Jared made his way there. "May I join you, Dr. Hussein?"

"Of course. Is your wife still sleeping also?"

"Yeah." Jared settled into a chair. "Was this a one-way trip, or will you be going back?"

"One way. We decided that five years was enough. And our first grandchild is due in three months. The second in five months. We want to be there for the milestones."

"I understand. Our son is getting married in a couple of weeks. But he and his wife are both hoping to be stationed on the moon. Our first grandchild might grow up there."

"I have often thought, when I saw parents with young children, that it must be very difficult for the grandparents. Even if they could afford to visit the moon, they cannot hold their grandchildren. They have to satisfy themselves with the one month a year when the family is on Earth."

"True. Where are you headed from here?"

"Egypt. We're spending two weeks visiting our parents and relatives before returning to our place in Florida. All of our children live there. And you?"

"Our ranch in New Mexico first. Then to Colorado for the wedding. We'll see a lot of relatives there. Home again, then on to Paris for meetings with Interpol before we head back here for quarantine."

"Partly a working vacation, then."

"Just a couple of days. I plan to enjoy myself until then."

Chapter 24

Jared sat on the porch of his ranch house with his feet up, mug of coffee in hand. Seventy-two hours on Earth had erased his fatigue, though he noticed more aches than he experienced on the moon—a normal response.

He liked the view from their piece of northern New Mexico even better than the one from their apartment on the moon. The ranch buildings sat on a level area on the side of a mountain. Beyond the porch the land dotted with shaggy-barked junipers sloped away gently, providing an awesome vista. Behind the buildings, the angle became steeper and pine trees outnumbered the junipers.

Karen's niece, Natalie, had aired out the house, turned on the water, and stocked the refrigerator before their arrival. They had not needed to leave the one hundred-sixty acre ranch yet. Natalie had also ridden their horses regularly. Today, they planned a short trail ride.

Rita's voice came through his earpiece. "Good morning, Chief. Are you enjoying your vacation?"

"Good morning, Rita. Yes, I am. What's up?"

"All is well here. Captain Julian asked that you call at your convenience."

"What time is it in Paris?"

"Four-fifteen PM."

"Call her."

The call connected somewhat faster than from the moon. "Jared, I was not certain that I would hear from you today."

"If I wasn't an early riser, you probably wouldn't have. It's six o'clock in the morning here. Has there been a development?"

"Oui. One you will not like. Pabaiga was found. He was not captured alive."

Jared sighed. "I guess I'm not surprised. He would have faced execution in at least a half-dozen countries. Have they found anything useful?"

"Highly encrypted computers, a cache of the poison, weapons of every kind. Work is progressing on the encryption. And you were correct. We found him in the city where the groundskeeper was killed."

"A lucky guess. Anything you want me to take a look at?"

"Lucky, he says. Nothing at this time. This is just an update. Enjoy your vacation."

"I plan to. I'll see you in about three weeks."

"Until then, mon ami."

***

Jared and Karen rode almost every day, increasing the distances until they were in shape for a long trail ride. They also enjoyed working on projects around the ranch. Jared repaired the roof on the chicken coop and all three of them added a half-mile of fence to the property.

During their second weekend on Earth, they accompanied Natalie into the Turkey Mountains for an overnight horse camping trip. Kayla and Kyle drove down from Denver to join them.

The following Thursday, Jared turned his pickup onto northbound Interstate 25, heading for Colorado Springs.

Karen studied the passing scenery. "All the you-and-me time and the wide open spaces have been just what I needed. But I'm ready to see some people again."

"We'll get plenty of them this weekend. By Sunday, I'll be ready for some fishing in the mountains."

"I'm glad Kayla and Kyle can take the extra day off so we get to spend more time with them. I just hope Kyle doesn't fall behind in his classes."

Jared patted her hand. "Don't worry. He's smart like his mom. Auto-pilot on." The computer took over. "Self-driving vehicles do make it easier to enjoy the scenery."

"But you'll take over when we get to Raton Pass."

"The computer is too cautious. I like to feel the curves. We haven't been back to the Academy since Joel graduated."

"Yes." She sounded wistful. "We'll miss Kyle's graduation unless we move our vacation next year."

"We can do that if he wants us to. Let's see how he feels about it."

"Okay. You really miss our home here, don't you."

"Yes. But probably no more than you do. Don't think that I hate living on the moon. It's like being a small town cop without having your hands tied. None of that, 'You can't arrest him because he's the mayor's son.' We have so many good friends there. We've owned the ranch six years and we barely know most of our neighbors."

Karen chuckled. "Even before we went to the moon, we weren't there enough. We were working out of San Diego."

"Two weeks a year and maybe a long weekend once in awhile. Now we get to spend the better part of a month. Sure, there are inconveniences that go with working on the moon, but we have it pretty good."

"We can afford to build that indoor arena Natalie wants."

"She's earned it. She takes really good care of the place. And her business is picking up. She's training four horses now and has three riding students. With the arena, it will be easier for her to keep working through the winter." He pointed. "Look. Elk."

They watched the four young bulls, each with two to three points on their antlers, grazing in a pasture.

Karen turned back toward him after they passed. "You might've missed that if you had been driving."

"I might have. Natalie and I will go over bids for the arena next week and pick a contractor. They should be able to finish before the weather gets too bad this winter."

"And you picked a location that won't obstruct our views."

"Believe me, that was the hardest part."

***

Jared, in dress uniform, and Karen greeted people as they entered the Air Force Academy chapel. Many of the guests wore International Air Force uniforms.

Two decades before, a number of countries had found the cost of maintaining their own air force and navy prohibitive. They had entered into a joint agreement with the United States. Twenty percent of airmen and sailors—like Wanda—came from these other countries.

Joseph Pearce sidled up to his son and nudged him with an elbow. "Pretty fancy duds, kid."

"Da-ad." Jared rolled his eyes like a teenager. "You know I gave away all my suits when I retired. This works for special occasions."

"And it fits right in with this crowd. I feel a little out of place."

"You feel out of place everywhere but the farm."

"Darned right."

"Joseph," Jeanette Pearce said while still ten feet away. "Let Jared do his job. It's time to take our seats."

Jared smiled. "Thanks, Mom. I'll talk to you after the service."

The last guests filed in, the music began, and the attendants— including Kyle and Kayla—joined both sets of parents in the back of the chapel. The groomsmen and bridesmaids entered together. Joel and Wanda came from side rooms.

Jared and Karen escorted Joel to the front of the chapel, then took their seats. Karen was already crying. Wanda came down the aisle flanked by Sara and Shin. The chaplain waited for her parents to find their spot, then began.

***

The sun took a long time to reach this mountain valley. Jared pulled on his waders in the dark and walked from the cabin's porch to the stream. He had his line in the water just as he could make out surrounding features.

Karen, Kayla, Kyle and Jared's parents were still asleep, recovering from the wedding celebration. *I can sleep in quarantine.* Jared chuckled. Boredom was a constant problem during those two weeks. Even with a movie theater, pool, and state-of-the-art gym, a person needed to have an extensive reading list before entering.

It's really the worst part of living on the moon. He understood the need for it. Despite all the air filters, a common cold would spread fast in the enclosed settlements. And taking something like Covid-19 there would be a disaster. Lunar medical facilities had limited Intensive Care units.

"Catching anything?" Joseph said behind him.

He smiled at his father, standing on shore, coffee cup in hand. "Not yet. Get a pole and try your luck."

"In awhile. I'm not quite as hardcore as you."

"You'd be hardcore too if you only got to fish for one month a year. You go year-round at home. Got one." Jared reeled in the trout and measured it against the top of his creel. He dropped it inside. "A few more and we'll have lunch."

"How about we hike over to the lake you told me about this afternoon so we can catch something besides trout?"

"Sounds good to me."

"Your mom and Karen are making breakfast. They said if you feel like eating it will be ready in a half-hour."

"If I'm not there, it's because they're really biting."

***

He missed breakfast. An hour later, Kyle came from the cabin while Jared cleaned his fish.

"Is that lunch?"

"Yes, it is. How's school?"

"Same old, same old. I'm sailing through most of my classes."

"Have you applied to vet schools?"

Kyle kicked the ground for a moment. "I wanted to talk to you and Mom about that. I'd like to take a year off. The veterinarian who takes care of our horses has agreed to hire me as a tech next spring."

Jared looked up. "And you think a year of experience as a vet tech will help you get into the school you want?"

"Yeah. And it will be good for me. I've been going to school since I was in Kindergarten. I've had part-time jobs, but I need to work for a year. I think I'll apply myself better when I go back to school."

"You have a point. Let's see what your mom has to say about it. On a related subject, do you want us to be here for your graduation next spring?"

"I've thought about that too. You can watch it from the moon. If I'm living at the ranch next September, we'll have a lot more quality time together. At graduation, I'll be too wound up to really enjoy your visit."

"Sounds good. And I think your mom will agree. Let's get these in the fridge. I'm ready for more coffee."

***

When the fishing trip ended, Jared and Karen said goodbye to their kids and his parents, then returned to the ranch. They had one day to themselves before her parents arrived, on their way from the wedding and visiting relatives to their home in Arizona.

After her parents left, Jared and Karen had two more days before they needed to leave for Paris. They sat on the porch their final morning.

Jared sighed. "You wouldn't have to go with me. You could spend more time here."

"And turn you loose with Renee? No, thank you." She laughed. "Seriously, I want to meet Rachelle. I can share a lot of memories of Henri with her."

"Okay. I'd rather stay here myself. But I just *had to* go after the big bucks and work for Interpol."

"Of course you only did it for *the money*. You're more content since you took that job. It was the right move."

"Yeah. It was. On a different subject, are you really okay with Kyle taking a year off?"

"He's not a kid anymore. He needs to make his own decisions. But I do think it's good for him to get out in the real world for a year. And, after working with a large animal vet, he may decide that he wants to be a small animal vet."

"I doubt it." Jared chuckled. "He's horse crazy."

"Like his parents. I have a surprise for you."

"Oh?"

"Wanda let it slip at the reception. She and Joel have put their applications in to NASA. They weren't planning to tell anybody."

Jared raised his eyebrows. "I thought they would at least wait until after they were married. With their experience, they should go to the top of the list of applicants. It would be great to have them so close. You know, they could even be stationed at Tranquility?"

"Were they planning to apply to be shuttle pilots? I never asked."

"He said that was their first choice, but they're qualified for other jobs."

"I'd better not get my hopes up. That's too much to expect. Still, if they were operating shuttles between settlements, we'd get to see them at least every couple of weeks." She grinned. "This is so exciting."

"Like you said, don't get your hopes up. There will be plenty of other qualified candidates."

Chapter 25

Early the next morning they flew out of Denver en route to Paris, with a layover in New York. They landed at de Gaulle Airport just after midnight, local time. A self-driving taxi took them to their hotel. By the time they checked in they were ready to sleep, even though they were still on New Mexico time—four PM.

Jared told the room's computer to wake them at eleven AM. He and Karen ate lunch at a bistro they had patronized on a previous trip, then took a human-driven taxi to Rachelle Le Claire's home.

She opened the door before he could ring the bell. "Thank you so much for coming." She gave them each a hug and a kiss on both cheeks. "Gaston and Jacques will join us in an hour. I wanted you to myself until then. Please, come in."

Jared recognized the room she led them to as the background he saw during their calls. "We have all the time we need. My meetings aren't till tomorrow morning."

"Please, sit. Can I get you a beverage?"

Karen smiled. "We're fine for now. We just finished lunch. You have a lovely home."

"Thank you. It is less than one-hundred, fifty years old, but it was built to match the historic buildings." She turned to Jared. "I know that you have been on vacation, but have you heard anything about the case."

"I'm probably no more up-to-date than you are. Did you hear on the news about the murderer-for-hire who was killed in Switzerland?"

"Yes. The reports said that he carried out most of the poisonings."

"That's right. When authorities decrypted his computer, they found payments from an account registered under a fake name. The woman who opened the account has done everything electronically for decades. The picture from the day she opened the account is of your mother with blonde hair."

"Please, don't call her that. She lost that right when she abandoned me. And she has done nothing but hurt me since."

"I understand. Have you been in contact with your sister?"

"Yes. We have talked by video several times. Her emotions are still very raw. I have helped her most by sharing memories of her father. And helping her understand that Michelle manipulated him, just like she did my father."

"Has talking to Victoria helped you?"

"Greatly. Helping her has helped me. And we have a number of things in common. She fills a void."

"Family."

"Exactly. My great-aunt and uncle have been gone for several years now. Losing them may be the reason I finally contacted Papa." She took a deep breath. "There is no doubt that Michelle killed Papa?"

"Not in my mind."

"We will not discuss it further. Tell me about him."

Jared smiled. "Henri was living his dream. I asked him once why he wanted to farm on the moon. He said that everything had already been done on Earth. He wanted to be a pioneer. And he was. He's credited with so many lunar agriculture firsts. When he arrived, almost all food was imported."

"He would not brag about himself, but I looked through the lunar news archives. He made headlines on a regular basis. Tell me things that didn't make the news."

"He could recognize rural people from the moment they stepped into the farm. He got along with everyone, but he was most comfortable with farm people. Within a week, I called him a friend."

Karen nodded. "I didn't get to spend as much time with him, so it took me a little longer. But he put me at ease. He also loved teaching kids about agriculture. Teachers brought their students to the farm at least once a week. And he helped them with their garden plots on other days. I heard him tell parents more than once to treasure their children. I know now that the advice came from losing you."

"I know that he loved me." Rachelle wiped her eyes. "It took me so long to get over my bitterness. I am grateful that it happened while he was still alive. I understand now that he did the right thing and that he could not take me with him. Michelle had a militia at her disposal. He had no choice." She shook her head. "I have been told that Papa had a seizure disorder."

"Yes," Jared said. "He had to keep it secret or he would have been Earthbound. That's how much his work meant to him."

"He will be remembered, no?"

"As long as there are settlements on the moon. There are a couple of projects in the works to assure that. The Tranquility farm will soon be designated the Henri Le Claire memorial farm. And there are plans to hold an annual lunar fair, like the county fairs held in some countries. The produce awards will be named for Henri."

"He would like that."

They visited with Rachelle until her husband and son joined them. Then all five continued the conversation in the backyard garden. Rachelle had inherited her father's gift with plants. Gaston excused himself to cook. After dinner, Jared and Karen rose to leave.

When they entered the foyer, Jared stopped in his tracks, staring at an object he had missed when they entered—a primitive sculpture of a falcon in flight. "That's an interesting piece. Where did you get it?"

"You may not believe this, but Michelle did that before I was born. It was in my aunt and uncle's house. It is the only thing I have from her."

Jared felt his heart begin to race. "That could be useful. May I take a picture of it?"

"Of course. But how could it help?"

Jared tapped the button camera on his lapel. "Maybe she still does sculpture. If we find a suspect, that could tell us if we're looking in the right direction. I know you don't want to talk about her, but did she have any mannerisms or habits that could help us identify her? Since we're sure she's had cosmetic surgery."

Rachelle's brow furrowed, then she nodded. "Yes. Perhaps. She laughed very loudly. But how useful will that be?"

"You never know." He met Karen's gaze and saw the shock in her eyes. "We'd better get back to our hotel and get some sleep. I have a long day tomorrow."

He took Karen's hand and they walked out to the street to another self-driving taxi.

Karen settled into the back seat. "Allison?"

"So I'm not crazy."

"When I noticed the sculpture, I thought that it looked kind of like her style. I would have never made the connection if you hadn't showed so much interest."

"I made the connection as soon as I saw it. The laugh confirmed it. Rita, call Captain Julian."

"Captain Julian is off duty. Should I call her personal number?"

"Yes, urgent."

Renee picked up almost immediately. "You have something?"

"I know the identity of Michelle Le Claire."

"Who? Where can we find her?"

"Her name is Allison Desjarlais. She's currently living on the moon."

Renee swore in French. "You are certain?"

"Pretty sure."

"Meet me at headquarters."

"I'll be there after I drop Karen off at our hotel."

***

Jared joined Renee in her office.

She gestured to a chair. "I have scanned the woman's records. Tell me why you suspect her."

"We just came from Rachelle Le Claire's home. Rita, send the sculpture pictures to Captain Julian's computer. When I saw this— even though it's pretty rough—I recognized her style."

The picture appeared on Renee's wall. "Computer show comparison photos of sculptures by Allison Desjarlais." The computer added images of three more sculptures. Renee nodded. "You have an eye for art, mon ami. Most people would not have been able to identify the artist from her early work."

"So you agree."

"No doubt. However, we need more before we can arrest her."

Jared smiled. "I have more."

"Go on."

"I asked Rachelle if her mother had any mannerisms that would help us identify her. She mentioned a loud laugh. I *know* Allison Desjarlais. One of the first things I noticed about her was her big laugh. And ... John Carter stopped in the Yukon town where she lived on one of his trips. And was at the same restaurant at the same time as Allison and her husband. I briefly considered her husband a suspect. Never thought to look at his wife. We also need to check her travel history against Philippe Fontaine's."

Renee leaned forward. "That is enough to arrest her and compel a DNA test. If she were on Earth, you and I would leave at once. How do we proceed?"

"I've been thinking about that since I figured this out. The woman is extremely dangerous. My people are competent and experienced, but logistics is the problem. They can lock her up at Tranquility. We could use a shuttle to transport her to Apennine, keeping her restrained. But then she would have to be loose to put on her suit for the flight to Earth. That's a risk I don't want to take."

"Where could she go? What could she do?"

"She couldn't really go anywhere. But she's an extremist, a sociopath who thought nothing of killing dozens of people and abandoning two daughters. She could decide to end it and take a lot of people with her in the process."

Renee shuddered. "I understand your reluctance to deal with her in a vacuum."

"And there's the matter of her husband. I have no idea if he's involved. And he's the head of Sequent Mining's lunar operation."

"At the very least, he could be difficult."

"And it would cause too much of an uproar. We need to wait till she returns to Earth. Another advantage is that she'll be safer to handle while she's adjusting to Earth's gravity."

"A wise precaution. How long before she returns to Earth?"

"She mentioned October. Rita, what are Allison Desjarlais' travel plans."

"Her flight to Earth is on October 5th," Rita said in his ear.

Jared relayed the information.

Renee smiled. "Eight days. Will her husband accompany her?"

"No. His vacation isn't for several months. She's planning to spend the time at their home in New Orleans."

"Do you have a plan for the arrest?"

"Let's see who else is on the flight. Rita, send the passenger manifest for the October 5th flight to Captain Julian."

When Renee displayed the passenger list, Jared slowly smiled. "We have a wild card. Amaya Ito is one of my officers. Since she lives at Taurus, there's very little chance that Allison would know that. I'll call her in the morning."

"And tell her what?"

Jared's brow furrowed. "Just to be ready for anything. Not to talk about her job to the other passengers. To bring along her immobilizer. I don't think I want to tell her that we plan to arrest Allison. Maybe just that we plan to make an arrest? I have till tomorrow morning to decide exactly what to say to her. Here's the plan I came up with on the way over here. I'm scheduled to go into quarantine in two days. If I don't go in on schedule, I'm afraid word will get back to the moon. The day Allison's flight lands, I come out and help you arrest her."

"Meaning you will not be able to return to the moon with your wife."

"I think in this case, she'll understand. This is important. I'll only be a couple weeks behind her."

"How will you deal with Michelle Le Claire's husband?"

"I won't tell my officers about this until she's en route to Earth. After we arrest her, I'll have them quietly detain Lloyd and I'll be the one to tell him what's going on. We need to try to figure out before then if he knows her true identity."

"And if he is innocent?"

"Unfortunately, he'll be another victim of this woman. I don't think his career will survive. Even if it does, I don't think he'll want to stay on the moon." Jared yawned. "It's like living in a small town."

"Best to lose yourself in a city. I am not certain if you can sleep, but return to your hotel. Come back an hour before your scheduled meeting."

"Sounds like a good idea. I'll see you then."

***

When Jared returned to the hotel, he found Karen waiting up for him.

She hugged him. "I love you. What's happening?"

"Allison is scheduled to return to Earth on the fifth. We'll arrest her in Houston."

"We'll be in quarantine by then."

"That's the plan. I have to go in so no one starts asking questions. But I'll have to leave when her ship is scheduled to land. I'm sorry, that means I'll be a couple weeks behind you going back. But I *need* to be there when she's arrested."

"Don't worry about it. Arresting a mass murderer is worth the couple weeks apart." She sat on the bed. "Arresting Henri's killer is even more important. It's a relief. I was hoping you had enough evidence to arrest her so I wouldn't have to face her again. That's all I've been thinking about since you dropped me off."

"I wouldn't ask you to do that. You have no poker face. She would suspect something as soon as she saw you."

Karen nodded at length. "I hope she has no reason to call me. Even that would give it away."

"Has she ever called you?"

"No. But still ..."

"Don't worry. If you hear her name on caller ID, don't answer."

"Right." She took a deep breath and let it out. "How are you handling this?"

"I'm angry." He clenched his fists. "Really ticked off. She had the audacity to *kiss my cheek.* After she killed my friend. I'd like to punch her in the face. *I* won't be able to hide how I feel. And I can't arrest her for eight days. I don't know *how* I'm going to sleep."

For the first time, Karen smiled. "I can help you with that."

Jared's shoulders dropped and he laughed. "Yeah, you can. You may regret making that offer."

"We'll deal with that if it happens."

Chapter 26

Jared slept fitfully, then rose early to call Amaya.

He caught her in her apartment. "Good morning, Chief. Are you calling from Paris?"

"Yes. I'm sure you weren't expecting to hear from me."

"No. You might call Lonnie, but you've never called me from Earth."

"It's about your vacation."

"O-kay."

"Have you been wearing your Earth vest?"

"Yes."

"Are you planning to bring your bull whip back here with you?"

"Why would I bring that?"

"I think you should. And have it in your carry-on pouch, all charged up."

"O-kay. Are you going to tell me why I'm doing this?"

"I'm not going to tell you details. We'll be arresting someone on your flight. Don't talk about your job to the other passengers. When you get into the ground vehicle, go toward the back so you'll be one of the last people off. When the person we're arresting sees us, I don't want them to be able to retreat inside."

"Okay. I understand. It will be like an undercover assignment. I can assume that the person you're arresting doesn't live at Taurus, because they all know I'm a cop."

"That's a valid assumption."

"Does anyone else on the team know about this?"

"Not yet. And I won't tell them until after your flight leaves."

"Understood. You can count on me, Chief."

"I knew I could. If there's anything else you need to know, I'll contact you."

***

The human-driven taxi stopped in front of Interpol headquarters later that morning.

Jared kissed Karen. "I can't believe you want to go to Notre Dame again."

"There's an exhibit about the fire in '19 and reconstruction. When I finish, I'll go to the Louvre."

"Okay. Enjoy yourself. I'll call when I get done." Jared entered the building and made his way to Renee's office. "Good morning. Any news?"

"Our superiors are not convinced that Allison Desjarlais and Michelle Le Claire are the same person."

"You must be joking." Jared dropped into a chair.

"Unfortunately, no. They asked why the fingerprints and DNA of the woman you know have never been flagged."

Jared threw up his hands. "When a person is declared dead, their DNA is removed from the active database. Anyone in law enforcement knows that. And, as Allison Desjarlais, she just turned in a DNA sample from someone else."

"I made that argument. What of the fingerprints?"

"Michelle was raised in an extremist group. She wasn't born in a hospital, never attended a public school, never had a driver's license, never held a job. None of the reasons average citizens get fingerprinted. And when she committed crimes, she wore gloves."

Renee smiled. "Thank you. I did not think of that. I will let you make the presentation at our meeting. Brigit will be here later today."

"What did you tell her?"

"Only that you identified Michelle Le Claire. Be prepared. She will probably kiss you."

"It's too soon to celebrate."

"Ah-h, contraire, mon ami. Our quarry has nowhere to go. She cannot hide on the moon. She can only return to Earth via official transport. And once she is in our custody, we will test her DNA, proving that she is Michelle Le Claire. There will be no bail for her. She will remain locked up until her execution."

"Keep telling me that."

"Come. It is time for our meeting."

***

Jared followed Renee into a conference room where he met for the first time in person their immediate superior and the director of Interpol. They took places at a table.

The director spoke. "Captain Julian has relayed to us that you are convinced not only that Michelle Le Claire is alive, but that she is responsible for the CV murders, *and* that she is living on the moon."

"Yes, ma'am."

"Convince me of the first premiss."

Jared leaned forward, his posture stiff. "She has a daughter born after the crackdown."

"You have never heard of freezing eggs and embryos?"

"Yes." Jared paused. *She's only playing devil's advocate.* "It's not something that could have been done in a CV clinic. If she had gone to a hospital, her fingerprints and DNA would have been recorded. Also, there is no record of a surrogate for Philippe Fontaine's first child. That can't happen. The only explanation is that he had an affair with a woman and the baby wasn't born in a hospital."

The director nodded. "Accepted. The second premiss?"

"Fontaine created the poison. But his confession that he killed because of 'survivor's guilt' doesn't hold water. A serial killer feeling guilty? Think about that. However, he was madly in love with Michelle Le Claire. He killed himself—chose a horrible death—rather than betray her. And one other thing. He killed Henri Le Claire, a man who left the CV ten years before the crackdown. A man who lived on *the moon*. There were a lot of easier targets who were spared. Why? Because the person with the real motive was Michelle Le Claire. The targets were people who either knew that she survived the crackdown or, like Henri, could identify her."

"Accepted. And your third premiss?"

"The motive for killing Henri. Michelle was coming to the moon. Even with cosmetic surgery, Henri would have exposed her. If nothing else, he would have identified her the way that I did. Her laugh. Her artwork. Also, the reason John Carter was murdered. Records placed him at a restaurant in Yukon at the same time as Michelle and her current husband. Carter recognized her. Many of the victims had travel to Canada in common. Other victims may have seen her right after the crackdown."

"And what of the remains found after the crackdown. This woman you know is not missing a finger."

"You've never heard of a prosthetic finger?"

The director smiled. "Captain Julian, has the computer analyzed the sculptures. Were they done by the same artist?"

"Yes. No doubt."

"Inspector Pearce, continue."

"I have no doubt that Michelle Le Claire and Allison Desjarlais are the same person. The safest course of action is to arrest her when she returns to Earth in seven days. A DNA test will confirm her identity."

The director nodded. "Your talent is wasted on the moon."

Jared leaned back in his chair. "My wife spent twenty years following me around the world. It's my turn."

"I understand. Do you intend to be present for the arrest?"

"Yes. I'll be in Houston anyway."

"She could choose another destination from Shepard Spaceport."

"No, she can't. Only tourists can. People who have resided on the moon—even temporary workers—have to go through Houston. There's a mandatory twenty-four hour hold and physical."

"I was not aware of that."

"That's why you have an inspector on the moon." Jared smiled.

"Captain Julian, thank you for submitting that suggestion. Select your team. Follow Inspector Pearce's instructions concerning procedure. Inspector, shall we move on to the other aspects of your job?"

***

The meeting continued until noon, then informally through lunch. Afterward, Jared and Renee returned to her office.

Brigit accosted him at the door and, as predicted, kissed him. The shock came when it landed on his lips. After an instant, he obliged her.

Brigit ended it, laughing. "I can do that. I am retired."

"I shouldn't do that. I'm married. But Karen will think it's funny."

"You can tell her tonight. I have made dinner reservations for the five of us. I owe both you and Renee this. I am vindicated."

"Well, thank you."

"Sit, sit." Renee waved them to chairs. "Brigit, I assume that you will join us in making the arrest."

"No one should attempt to keep me away."

"I thought so. Jared, there is still the matter of Lloyd Desjarlais. All indications are that he has no knowledge of his wife's true identity. He met her a year after the birth of her second daughter. Each time she rendezvoused with Fontaine, she used an arts function to explain her travel."

"I feel kind of sorry for him. He seems like a decent guy. And I think he's madly in love with her too."

"We know of three men who succumbed to her spell. It is her children who will truly suffer. She has twin sons with this Desjarlais, nineteen years old. This will be a crushing blow for them."

"I've heard Lloyd talk about them. He's a good father. That's another reason he'll leave the moon. And it's too bad because he's been an asset. That woman is pure evil. She's hurt so many people in so many ways besides murder."

Brigit extended her hands toward him. "Thank you. I felt that from the time I was assigned to the CV case. Others saw her sympathetically, a victim of her father's fanaticism. To me, she seemed to relish cold-blooded murder. She liked to watch her victims die. It certainly surprises me that she was able to hide those qualities for so many years."

"I suppose I shouldn't feel so angry that she was able to fool me." He shrugged. "She had lots of practice."

"A chameleon," Renee said. "Willing to do anything to survive. I am grateful that we will be able to arrest her in a weakened state from living in low gravity."

"Just bring me a gun. I don't want to face her without one and mine are all at the ranch."

Chapter 27

The following morning, Jared and Karen flew to Houston. They enjoyed a few hours in the city before checking into a NASA hotel, then reporting to quarantine the next morning. After a physical, they entered the isolation area.

Jared tried to follow his usual first day schedule of visiting with newcomers, teaching them the ropes. This time he found himself distracted. *I need a "project" to keep me occupied. Someone who seems especially nervous.*

He zeroed in on a wide-eyed woman of about forty, sitting at a table alone. He smiled. "First trip to the moon?"

"Everybody keeps asking me that. How can you tell?"

"You look scared to death."

"I am." She let her breath out. "I keep wondering if I've made a huge mistake."

"They *did* tell you that you can back out anytime before your flight?"

"Yes. I need the money. If I can just work there for a year, I'll get back on my feet."

"That's a pretty common reason. I only went there because my wife wanted to." He flashed another smile. "I was terrified for about three months. You get used to it. It's not a bad place to live."

"What do you do there?"

"I'm Jared Pearce." He extended his hand. "The police chief. So believe me when I tell you that you probably won't live anywhere with a lower crime rate."

She shook his hand. "I'm Sue Flemming. Wait. I heard there was a murder a few months ago."

"There was. But it turned out he was given the poison on Earth. So you don't have to worry about crime. What's your job?"

"Environmental Control. I'll be manning the computers for all the life-support systems."

"Valuable work. Which settlement?"

"Tranquility."

"I'll be seeing you around then. That's where I live. As someone who has spent four years there, take my advice. Try to relax and enjoy this. People pay a lot of money to go on this kind of adventure. You're not only getting your trip paid for, but you'll be making a bundle."

She gave a nervous laugh. "Thanks. I feel a little better."

***

Jared used that strategy for the next five days. He and Karen reassured Sue and two other newcomers who seemed nervous.

On the morning Jared left quarantine to meet Allison/Michelle's flight, Sue joined Karen at the breakfast table. "Where's your husband?"

"His job interfered. He'll have to catch the next flight." Karen smiled at Sue's concerned expression. "Don't worry. I'll get you through this."

Meanwhile, in the arrival building, Jared met with Renee, Brigit, two FBI agents, and NASA's head of security. He had chosen to wear a shirt identifying his department and rank, though Renee introduced him as "Inspector Pearce, Lunar Enforcement Chief."

"You have the warrant?" Jared asked.

Renee removed it from her pocket. "All in order."

He addressed the NASA officer. "Where's the flight now?"

"At Shepard. Passengers are transferring. They should land in less than an hour."

"The best time to arrest her will be when she gets off the bus in the garage here. She will have her spacesuit off so there will be nothing to interfere with shackling her. She'll also be at her weakest from Earth's gravity. Even if she wanted to try something, she'll be pretty helpless."

"I bow to your experience," Renee said. "I would have grabbed her as soon as the shuttle landed."

With the exception of the NASA officer, the others nodded.

Jared turned to the female FBI agent. "You have a secure lockup ready for her?"

"It's waiting outside. The latest thing. Made from the same polymer as your lunar habitats. Once she's in there, she doesn't come out till trial. No risky transfers. She's moved everywhere in her cube. It's only used for the most dangerous criminals."

"Sounds good to me. We'll stay in this room until the transport vehicle goes out to meet the shuttle. I'm not taking any chances that someone will let something slip."

***

Jared and the others waited in the air-conditioned garage with guns drawn but pointed down. A wide-eyed driver pulled the transport in and began lowering it while the garage doors closed. Jared disbursed his team so they could not be seen by those inside the transport until they reached the doorway.

Jared knew everyone on the flight. He held a finger to his lips, then waved for each of the first three people to keep moving. A smiling Michelle reached the door fourth.

The law enforcement officers all raised their weapons.

Her smile vanished.

Jared's voice almost quivered with anger. "Michelle Le Claire, you're under arrest for murder and crimes against humanity."

She made no attempt to deny it. There was no sign of the charming act she had mastered. Cold, hard eyes looked from one member of the assembly to the next, pausing on Brigit, before coming to rest on Jared.

"Do you think you have enough people?" She crossed her hands in front of her.

Jared's weapon shook. "You shouldn't have killed my friend."

She shrugged. "I should have divorced Lloyd when he suggested the stupid idea of transferring to the moon. I was quite thorough removing everyone who knew of me. How did you discover my identity?"

"Rachelle kept one of your sculptures."

"Ah-h." She raised her eyebrows. "And you have an eye for art. I should have killed her too."

Jared could not hide his loathing. "Cuff her."

The FBI agents approached her. The male agent extended shackles toward her crossed hands. Her left hand shot out and the man convulsed and fell backward. Another lightning move and the female agent was on the floor also.

Michelle reached back into the vehicle and jerked a woman out, using her as a human shield. Jared recognized Doreen, the store clerk. Michelle pressed the little finger of her left hand to the woman's carotid artery.

"Those two will recover." She nodded to the downed agents. "She won't if I discharge my weapon into her neck."

Jared's knuckles turned white on his pistol. "Let her go!"

"No. Now we negociate." Michelle took a step back. "I have her and the rest of these hostages. Get me a ride out of here."

"If you kill her, we shoot you."

Michelle stepped back again. "She's your friend, Chief. Everyone is your friend. You don't want to be responsible for her death."

One more step. "Let her go!"

Michelle laughed and backed up one more time.

Amaya's immobilizer shot out, encircling both Michelle and Doreen. They became rigid and fell through the doorway.

Jared rushed in and dragged Michelle away from Doreen. He flipped her face down, shoved a knee against her back, then grabbed the little finger of her left hand. He wrenched the weapon off, leaving a bloody wound.

He looked up, panting. Renee offered him handcuffs.

"Thanks." He holstered his weapon, then cuffed Michelle's hands behind her back.

The NASA security agent applied shackles to her ankles.

Only then did Jared climb off her. He took a deep breath to slow his pounding heart.

Amaya stood in the doorway, retracting her immobilizer. "She killed Henri?"

"She ordered it. Congratulations on your promotion, Sergeant."

Amaya grinned. "Thanks, Chief. But I'd give her another shot if you'd let me."

"If it were just me and you, I *might* let you." He helped Doreen up. "Sorry about that. It was the safest way to subdue her."

She swayed, grabbing his arm for stability. "I don't care. I've never been so afraid in my life."

"I'll get one of the ground crew to help you." He handed her off and helped up the two FBI agents.

They all watched Renee press a DNA scanner against Michelle's scalp. It returned the analysis in less than two minutes. Renee smiled. "Identity confirmed."

Jared just nodded. He and Renee dragged a glaring Michelle to her feet, then pushed her at the shuffling pace dictated by the shackles.

The agents led the way to her cubicle. It sat in the back of a truck, furnished like any other jail cell. The agents stepped onto a lift with the prisoner, rode up, then locked her inside without removing the shackles.

Renee squeezed Jared's arm. "Are you coming with us while we process her?"

"No. I'll see you later. I need to talk to Lloyd, then I want to be the one to tell my citizens."

"I understand."

Jared returned to the room where they had planned the arrest and sat at the desk. "Rita, send a message to Karen. 'She's in custody.' Do my officers have Lloyd?"

"Yes, Chief. He is waiting in your office."

"Connect me to Halolani."

"Connecting to Lieutenant Makai."

"I'm here, Chief."

"Rita, on screen."

Lloyd appeared, creases in his brow, sitting in Jared's chair with Halolani standing beside him. "Chief! What's wrong? Has something happened to Allison?"

"Lloyd, there's no easy way to say this. We've arrested the woman we all knew as Allison. DNA has confirmed that she is the wanted killer and terrorist Michelle Le Claire."

Lloyd made a choking sound, then sagged. He propped himself on the desk. "No. We've been married twenty years. I would have known."

"Not unless she wanted you to. She's spent her whole life deceiving people. And she knew how to make a man fall in love with her."

Lloyd stared for a moment. "Le Claire. That's the name of the man who was murdered."

"Henri was her first husband. She knew that he would recognize her despite the cosmetic surgery. He was in her way."

"She only came here because of me. She must have loved me to do that."

"No, Lloyd. You were just a means to get what she wanted. The woman isn't capable of loving."

"But she was a good mom. She loves our boys."

"I'm sorry, Lloyd. Everyone was a pawn to her. She had your children to keep you hooked. She took care of them to endear herself to you. She had two daughters before she met you, to keep their fathers under her control. When it suited her, she abandoned them."

"I just can't believe it. There must be some good in her. I need to stand by her."

"Lloyd, I don't want you to destroy your life. You need to hear it in her own words. Rita, play the footage of Michelle Le Claire's arrest from my camera."

Jared watched Lloyd and listened to the recording. Tears began rolling down Lloyd's cheeks. He collapsed on the desk with his head on his arms, sobbing. Halolani rubbed her hand over his back.

It took a couple of minutes for him to regain his composure. He sat up and wiped his eyes. "How do I tell my sons?"

"There's no easy way to do it. The thing is, this will be the headline for every news agency by this evening. They need to hear it from you."

Lloyd nodded. "I need to be with them."

"I'll arrange a shuttle to take you to Apennine. You can be on tomorrow's flight. One of my officers will be with you until you leave for Earth."

"Thank you, Jared. I don't deserve your kindness. My decisions caused the death of your friend."

"You're *not* responsible, Lloyd. She likes killing. And I'm sure if she had objected too much, you wouldn't have taken the job. Right?"

"Yes. She tried to talk me out of it, but not for long."

"Right. She wanted to come there too and was willing to kill a lot of people who might recognize her when she appeared on the news."

Lloyd shook his head. "How could I not know?"

"I didn't know, Lloyd. She was just *that* skilled at fooling people."

"Maybe. Thank you for everything. I'd better get ready to travel."

"Rita, end call. Connect me to Halolani."

"I'm here, Chief."

"I'll call transportation services and tell them to have a shuttle on standby. When Lloyd's ready to travel, tell them and they should be prepared to leave within minutes. Send somebody with him. Then have somebody on the dark side stay with him until his flight. He's pretty fragile right now."

"I'll take care of it, Chief."

"I probably have an hour before this news breaks. I need to contact Regina so people there get the story from me."

"The good thing is, most people will be in bed before it breaks. They won't get the news till morning. It won't be easy no matter how they hear it, but it'll be best that way. You have a calming affect on people, Chief."

"Thanks, I'll talk to you later."

Chapter 28

Jared reached Regina Gonzales at her apartment, wearing a sweatshirt and no makeup, her usually coifed hair loose on her shoulders.

"Chief, this must be major for you to call me from quarantine."

"I had to come out of quarantine. That's how major it is."

"Wow. Let me know when you're ready to record."

"Not yet. You need some time to absorb this. We've arrested Allison Desjarlais—"

"Holy sh ... Pardon my French. Why?"

"Her real name is Michelle Le Claire. She's the CV killer."

"She killed Henri?"

"Yes, and dozens of other people."

"Did Mr. Desjarlais know?"

"He had no idea. She was that good at fooling people. He'll be on his way back to Earth in the morning to be with his sons. I'm ready to make a statement for the citizens and you can fill in your part later."

"Turning record on."

"Hello, friends. I need to share shocking news with you. Today I—with the cooperation of Interpol, the FBI, and NASA security—arrested the woman we knew as Allison Desjarlais upon her return to Earth. DNA has confirmed what we believed. She is Michelle Le Claire, a murderer and terrorist thought long dead. She is responsible for the CV killings, including the murder of our friend, Henri Le Claire. He was her first husband.

"Lloyd Desjarlais was not involved in any of this. He is returning to Earth to be with his sons during this difficult time. They need your prayers.

"You will be hearing a lot about this on the news over the next few days. I wanted you to hear it from me first." He paused. "End recording."

"Record off. Are you okay, Chief?"

"Just tired. I've been working on this case for months, but I don't feel like celebrating."

"This stinks. I kind of liked her."

"I did too. She was very good at fooling people. Look up Michelle Le Claire before you go on in the morning. She enjoyed killing. She is a very bad person."

"I will. I may have more questions for you in the next few days."

"Leave me a message. I'll get back to you. Rita, end call. Send a message to Rachelle Le Claire. 'We caught her. You have more siblings. Twin brothers, age nineteen. Call me when you're ready.' End message.

***

Jared requested a ride to the quarantine building and spoke to Karen through glass. NASA had gone out of its way to make this not feel like visiting a prisoner. They sat in comfortable chairs in a private room.

He rubbed his hands over his face. "I won't be able to come in until you leave, so I think I'll go to the ranch for a few days."

"Do you want me to come out?"

Jared stared at her for a moment. "I won't ask you to. With Lloyd leaving, Sequent needs its head geologist more than ever. Right?"

"Right. Still, I'd like to be there for you."

"I appreciate that. But I just feel like I've run a marathon. I did what I promised. I caught Henri's killer. I may start to feel good about that tomorrow."

"You should."

"You know the stupid thing that keeps running through my mind?"

"What to do with her sculpture?"

He flashed a quick smile. "You know me so well. I'm not sure I want it in our apartment anymore."

"I'll ship it back to the ranch."

"I'm not sure I want it there either."

"That's where it's going for now. All her work will be worth more because of her notoriety. Think about how valuable *that* sculpture will be if we wait awhile to sell it. Artwork by an infamous criminal once owned by the man who caught her."

"Your mind just works different than mine. I wouldn't feel comfortable making a profit from something that was a gift."

"You can donate it to charity. For now, we're keeping the sculpture."

"Okay. You win. But ship it as soon as you get back. I don't want to see it for awhile."

"I'll take care of it." She gazed at him with loving eyes. "It's all over but the paperwork."

One corner of his mouth turned up. "Don't remind me. I need to head over to the FBI field office now to work on that and talk to Renee."

"Tell Brigit no more kisses."

Chuckling, he stood, kissed his fingers, and touched the glass. "I love you."

Karen kissed her fingers and touched the other side. "I love you."

"We'll spend more time together tomorrow. I'll see you then."

***

After letting Renee know that he was on his way, Jared took a taxi to the FBI field office.

She met him at the door. "I heard several favorable comments concerning your insistence that we arrest her upon her arrival. She could have caused considerable damage if she had been at full strength."

"It's just common sense. I've always felt pretty vulnerable for a couple days after returning to Earth."

"If you go to see her again, I warn you to expect verbal abuse."

"That won't happen until her trial. I have no desire to see her."

"You should be able to do that without returning to Earth. Do you think she is a suicide risk?"

"No. She thinks too much of herself. The risk is that she'll keep trying to escape until she's executed. No one should ever be alone with her. She's seduced three men. One of them killed himself rather than risk betraying her." He let Renee think about that for a moment.

She led him into a conference room where Brigit waited.

Renee nodded. "You are correct. I will give the order." She turned to Brigit. "Jared believes that no one should be alone with Michelle."

"My thoughts exactly. We dare not underestimate that fiend."

"And, now, our favorite part of police work. Reports."

Jared smiled. "You know, maybe for the first time in my career, I don't mind."

###

Other books by the author

TONY WAGNER MYSTERIES

The Reverend Finds His Calling

The Reverend Goes Home

The Reverend, Meth, & Murder

The Reverend: Murder In Medora

The Reverend Delivers

The Reverend Down East

The Reverend: AKA Wohanota

The Reverend & the Lady in Sand

The Reverend & the Kidnapped Girl

The Reverend Finds His Way

RANDY MCKAY MYSTERIES

Silent Stranger

Rewriting History

Coming in 2021: *Written In Smoke*

FOR YOUNGER READERS

Gold Star Lee

ROMANCES

Greener Pastures

Wrong Turn

Right Hand Man

COLLINS FAMILY SAGA

Royal Entanglements

Cowboy Prince

Collins Family Reunion

James Collins: Crash!

About the Author

A native of North Dakota, Paula F (Pfeiffer) Winskye began writing stories about girls & horses at age 12. For 30 years, she wrote for her own enjoyment, until her husband John encouraged her to seek publication.

She self-published her first novel in 2003. *Murder At Taurus* is her 21st.

2007 saw the publication of her first mystery, *The Reverend Finds His Calling,* the initial Tony Wagner novel. The series has grown to ten volumes. She has released two in her Randy McKay series, and will publish the third in 2021.

Her other books include three romances, four volumes in the Collins Family saga, and a middle grade novel, *Gold Star Lee.*

Winskye is a member of the Sisters in Crime and its Tucson chapter.

She and John live near Snowflake, Arizona where she is a Navajo County Sheriff's Auxiliary Volunteer.

Learn more at: www. winskyebooks. com

On Facebook: Follow Author Paula F. Winskye

On Twitter: @Awinskye

Made in the USA
San Bernardino, CA
14 June 2020

72976546R00163